# STICKY FINGERS 3

JT LAWRENCE

FIRE FINCH

# ALSO BY JT LAWRENCE

## FICTION

WHEN TOMORROW CALLS
• *SERIES* •

The Stepford Florist: A Novelette (Oct 2017)

The Sigma Surrogate (2018)

1. Why You Were Taken (2015)

2. How We Found You (May 2017)

3. What Have We Done (October 2017)

## STANDALONE NOVELS

The Memory of Water (2011)

Grey Magic (2016)

## SHORT STORY COLLECTIONS

Sticky Fingers (2016)

Sticky Fingers 2 (2018)

Sticky Fingers 3 (2018)

## NON-FICTION

The Underachieving Ovary (2016)

# DEDICATION

# STICKY FINGERS 3

JT LAWRENCE

# CONTENTS

1. Tears of a Dead Man                                    1
2. Sky Mirror                                              9
3. The Shelter                                            33
4. The Children in the Walls                              77
5. Death is a Woman in a Blue Dress                       87
6. Fenrir                                                 91
7. Lucky Strike                                          107
8. The Hostage Situation                                 117
9. Every Breath You Take                                 123
10. Memory, Mirrors, and the World Inside My Head        161
11. Blackwater Estuary                                   173
12. Perky Pilgrim                                        197

*Acknowledgments*                                        217
*About the Author*                                       219
*Dear Reader*                                            221

# 1

## TEARS OF A DEAD MAN

"WHAT SEEMS TO BE THE PROBLEM?" asks the doctor.

He's young—too young—and he's wearing an expensive scarf. Two clues that he doesn't really know anything. I'm not saying he didn't go to med school. I'm not saying the certificates on the wall are fake.

"Mister Rohandron?" he says. "What can I help you with today?"

I stare at the paisley pattern on the green silk wound around his neck. It reminds me of a snake. I heave my eyes up to his.

"I think I'm dead," I say.


Doctor Folly—

(Folly? Really? And he expects me to take him seriously as a man of science? But there is his surname up on the wall, in gold, and I suppose there is no arguing with that.)

Doctor Folly purses his lips, and his adam's apple moves up and down. It's a knobbly one, and it makes me wonder how he gets such a clean shave over that jagged rock of cartilage. Makes me wonder how he—in a hurry for a medical conference—doesn't slip and cut the whole thing off and bleed to death in his luxurious en-suite bathroom.

"You think you're dead?"

Why is he repeating after me? Does he think he misheard? Did he think I said I *think I'm deaf*?

"Yes," I say. "I think I am dead."

His dark eyebrows link together. He's got a deep frown for a man of such a tender age.

"All right," he says, tilting his head slightly. "What makes you think that?"

"Can you do the exam?" I ask. "Do the physical examination and then we'll talk later."

Doctor Folly blinks at me.

"All right," he says again.

He taps his stethoscope with a manicured finger, then places the cold disc—a silver grey planet—on my chest. He's still frowning.

"Breathe in," he says, and I do.

"Breathe out."

The air leaves my chest in a rush. My lungs still work. They still balloon and shrink, balloon and shrink, but it's dead air.

Dr Folly listens as I examine the creases in his forehead. There aren't very many; not compared to mine, anyway. My skin is a stinking shroud, a roadmap to nowhere etched in dead leather.

He removes the planet from my chest and shrugs his stethoscope back around his neck.

"You see?" I say, buttoning up my shirt. "Dead inside."

"Mr Rohandron," he says, "as far as I can tell, you're very much alive."

I'm incensed. I'm tired of doctors who think they know more about my body than I do after an examination that took less than sixty seconds. "What kind of medical exam was that?"

"You are breathing, Mr Rohandron," says the man.

"It's dead air," I say. "It's not reaching my bloodstream."

"And your heart is beating."

"Don't you think I'd know if my heart was beating?"

I lie awake at night clutching my chest, hoping for a heartbeat, willing it to pulse, but it does not comply.

Dr Folly offers me his stethoscope but I wave it away. I won't fall for his doctors' tricks. I refuse to be mesmerised by a planet on the end of a string.

He sits down in his chair and swivels it to face me directly. "What do you want from me, then?"

"A death certificate," I say.

He doesn't break eye contact. "Why?"

"I'm ready to move on. My body will be stuck here until I pass into the next world."

Who knows if there is a next world? Not me. But either way, I'm tired of living in a dead man's limbo.

"Mr Rohandron. You are living and breathing. Dead men can't walk into doctors' offices."

"I realise it defies logic," I say. "But that's how things are, sometimes."

"Do you *want* to die?"

I blink at him. His question comes two weeks late. Two weeks ago I took a toaster into the bath with me because I wanted to die. I'd rather be alive now but it's too late. My brain is dead and my organs have melted: my intestines are soup. I reek of death. Can't he smell that disgusting sweet-sour scent of rotting flesh on me? Summer roadkill and roadside weeds. Eshana's perfume. I can't escape the stench; it's in my nostrils all the time.

"I want to be with other dead people," I say.

I would go ahead and bury myself if I wasn't afraid of closed spaces. Instead I bought an expensive mahogany coffin and keep it in my lounge at home. When I get anxious I run my hands over the polished wood and that makes me feel better.

"Tell me how you feel," says the doctor, pushing his neat spectacles up the bridge of his nose.

I bite my lips—chew them hard—but it doesn't hurt.

"Numb," I say, "as if my body is fading away."

"Like a ghost?"

My eyes snap into his. How does he know? "Yes. Like a ghost."

"You've lost your appetite," he says.

I know my face is gaunt. My skeleton is emerging because I am dead. That is the way it goes.

"There's no point in eating," I say. "When you're dead."

"Perhaps that fading feeling is because you haven't eaten."

"It's not."

"When last did you have a meal?"

"Just before I died. Two weeks ago."

There is a bloom of colour in the doctor's cheeks, and he loosens the green silk snake from around his neck.

"Mr Rohandron. You are starving yourself. That is why you feel ill."

"No," I shake my head. "You are missing the point."

"With all due respect, Mr Rohandron, I think it is you who is missing the point. You will die if you don't begin eating again."

This man just doesn't get it. What will happen to the food? My stomach is a scorched stone. Food is not the answer.

"Let me book you into hospital," he says. "You don't have to eat anything. We'll give you an IV until you feel better. Perhaps you just need some rest."

"I hear my wife's voice calling me," I say. "Even though she lives three thousand miles away. It's like she's in the next room."

"Your wife? Did she leave you? Is that what—"

"She went home to India."

"Is that perhaps what has caused this ... episode?"

I don't reply.

"Do you have a history of depression, Mr Rohandron? A bi-polar diagnosis? Do you have a psychologist?"

"What good is seeing a psychologist?" I ask him. "My brain is dead. I'd rather sit in a graveyard."

It's not a throwaway figure of speech. Graveyards are the only place I feel comfortable. Leaning against a tombstone is even better than spending time in my lounge with the lacquered casket. It's less lonely. I was even thinking that a morgue would be a good place to be, but, again, I worry about the claustrophobia of those pull-out fridge beds.

"Would you give me permission to phone your wife in India? We can discuss the situation with her. Perhaps we can gain some perspective. Or perhaps she'll come back to see you."

"Eshana won't believe you," I say. "She won't believe that I'm dead."

He looks at me, abrading my numb skin with his focused gaze.

"You died two weeks ago?"

"Yes," I say. "I'm just waiting for the rest of my body to catch up."

"Catch up?"

"Shrivel up and reveal my skeleton."

"And your wife is ... *alive?*"

I have to think about this. Yes. She is alive. I think she is alive.

"If I type her name into my computer here," he says, motioning at the silver laptop on his desk. "Will her death notice come up?"

I have to think about this one.

"Is your wife really in India, Mr Rohandron?"

"That's where I like to picture her," I say. I see Eshana wearing a saffron sari and there are marigolds, their petals edged with flames. But she's not standing and smiling. She's lying down on a timber raft with her eyes closed, her arms crossed at her chest. She's covered in flowers of fire.

Seeing the flames in my mind's eye causes my own chest to burn, and I strike it hard and cough. My lungs will soon be melted, too, and maybe then I'll get that death certificate.

"How did your wife die, Mr Rohandron?" he asks. There is some perspiration on his upper lip. I don't perspire anymore. Dead men don't sweat.

I'm about to say Eshana didn't die. Eshana is alive. But then I see her as if she is in the room with us, and the bright yellow sari blasts us with its saffron light. Then she's on the raft again, buried in marigold petals and sweet smoke. Then she's lying in that coffin I bought, her skin melting away more each day, filling the air with the stench of regret. The smell I can't escape.

Tears roll down my face. Tears from where? Who knows how a

dead man can cry, but there is no denying the warm splashes on my hollow cheeks.

Dr Folly stands up and moves closer, to comfort me, but I hold up a hand for him to keep his distance. I weep into the crook of my bony arm. There's nothing saltier than tears of a dead man.

Eshana was the one who took the toaster into the bath with her. I was too late. I couldn't save her, but I died trying.

# 2

## SKY MIRROR

ROBIN SUSMAN THROWS her dirty laundry into her scuffed suitcase. She nicks the small bar of complimentary hotel hand soap, still neatly wrapped in its shiny, pleated paper, and throws that in, too. She'll put it in her guest bathroom when she gets home. Not that she ever receives any guests. The twin shotguns she keeps at the front door have proven a reliable deterrent.

Maybe she'll give it to Liz, the lady who cleans her house. Where Robin lives, on a small sheep farm in the Free State, a bar of soap will not go to waste.

There's a knock on the door. Probably housekeeping. She still needs two minutes to finish packing.

"Two minutes!" yells Susman.

She's running late, but at least she doesn't have a flight to catch; flights always make her nervous. She's looking forward to the drive. Four and a half hours of crisp blue sky, out of the smog-grimy city and on to the skinny sun-grilled roads and red hills of her home.

There is more knocking on her hotel room door; slightly more insistent now.

Robin can almost smell the scent of lamb's wool, the hot baked sand, the grassy baled hay. She pictures the still water of the dam: a sky-mirror shot through with reeds.

She squashes down the lid of the suitcase and zips it up, catching the hem of a crumpled T-shirt as she does so.

*Bugger.*

"Susman," says the person on the other side of the door; a voice she immediately recognises. Robin stops fussing with the stuck zip and walks to the door.

She opens it, and her skew smile fades. "What's wrong?"

Detective de Villiers is out of breath and sweating.

"Has something happened?"

He looks at her and she stares back; his kind blue eyes corrupted by the things he has seen.

Eventually he says: "You're not going to like this."

"No," she says. "The answer is *no.*"

"Just give me a couple of minutes to—"

"Forget it, Devil. I'm not staying."

She leaves him standing at the door and walks back to her suitcase, forcing the small handle of the zip past the cotton caught in its silver teeth. She derails the zip and tears her thumbnail at the same time. Her jaw muscles hum with frustration and fury.

"Can I help with that?" asks de Villiers.

*It'll never close, now. It's ruined.*

"Damn you," says Robin, through clenched teeth. She sucks her torn nail, ripped right down to the quick, and tastes the copper tint of blood.

"Damn you," she says again, and slams the luggage onto the floor.

De Villiers looks at her. "Was that directed at me, or your suitcase?"

She spins round, ready to give him a piece of her mind, but sees him flinch, and stops. He was ready to duck, as if he had been expecting her to throw something at him.

In her mind she sees the old hotel glass tumbler flying through the air, missing the detective by a millimetre—in slow motion— then exploding into crystal shards on the cream wallpaper behind him.

Her heart softens. "How are things at home, Devil?"

De Villiers' eyes spark, then he looks at the carpet and shrugs the question off, clears his throat.

"We need you," he says.

Her arms fall to her sides. "I just want to go home."

"Just one more day," he says.

11

"I need to be on the farm," says Susman. "I can't breathe here. I can't sleep."

If she were to be completely honest, she'd say that it's not that she *can't* sleep in this city, it's more that she *doesn't want* to sleep. It seems that when she's asleep in Jozi her demons know exactly where to find her; she can't stand the idea of even one more night waking up in a pool of perspiration, voice hoarse, heart beating on the ceiling above, her manic fingers scratching wildly against an invisible assailant.

"I know it's difficult for you," he says.

Robin coughs a laugh, bitter as tar. "Difficult?"

"It's hell. It must be hell. I get it. But there's a woman missing."

"There is always a woman missing," says Robin. "Hundreds of thousands of women missing. I can't save them all, and nor can you."

"Maybe we can save this one."

*Why? Why this one?* she wants to ask, but she already knows that Devil won't have an answer, except to say that she's a woman who needs their help. And he knows his best shot of finding her is with Susman.

Robin's eyes well up with tears of frustration, and another emotion that she can't quite place. A mixture of grief and regret, but something more than that. It hovers around her; haunts her.

She takes a deep breath and blinks the tears away.

"I understand if you can't do it," he says, but they both know he won't. "I'm on my way to the station now for a briefing."

Robin sighs and kicks her suitcase.

"Let's get some decent coffee, first," she says, sniffing and swiping away the remainder of her emotion with the edge of her sleeve. "You're buying."

Susman carries the three still-hot take-away cups into the police station. Khaya jumps up when he sees her and she almost drops the coffee.

"You're back!"

"I never left," she grumbles, passing him a cup. She looks at Blom's perennially tidy workspace. It always worries her. "Where's the Flying Dutchman?"

"Family emergency," says Khaya.

Robin looks at the coffee and shrugs. "More for me."

"My office, now!" yells de Villiers.

"Jesus, Devil, you don't need to shout."

He shoots them a look. His arms are full of files so he kicks his wheeled chair into place, dumps them onto his desk, and sits down.

"It's the caffeine," whispers Khaya to Robin. "He's trying to cut down. It makes him jumpy."

"It's his personality disorder that makes him jumpy," says Robin.

Khaya smiles at her. "I'm so glad you're back."

Robin turns to walk to Devil's office. "I'm not back."

"April Mixon," says de Villiers. "Last seen alive at a filling station close to her home in Mondeor, before leaving for Glenmore, in Durban. Security cam footage confirms the credit card transaction at 10:28."

"What's in Durban?" asks Susman.

"Business. She's an IT rep at Swift and works from both offices when she needs to."

"I don't get it," says Khaya.

"What?"

"She's works for one of the biggest IT companies in the country, but they don't use video-conferencing?"

"Not everything can be done over the airwaves, Khaya."

"Give me one example."

Devil's phone rings. "De Villiers," he says into the receiver, and then the creases in his forehead deepen. "Oh," he says. "Okay," and puts down the phone.

Susman and Khaya look at him, waiting for the bad news they know is coming.

"They found her car. A Mazda2 hatchback. Or, at least, they found the signal from her car. She has a transponder. Bottom of Lake Asha, 128km from Durban city. Local guys are on their way. "

· · ·

14

"Let's hope they stripped the transponder off the car and threw it into the lake," says Robin. The alternative chills her, so she tries to push the thought away, but it doesn't work. All of a sudden she's in the hatchback as it rolls slowly into the water, the tyres trudging trenches into the sucking mud. She can't move, can't reach to unclip her safety belt. The car seat is firm on her back and her legs are numb. The water rushes in: first through the front of the car, weighing it down, pulling it further into the lake, then it cascades through the open windows, sloshing down the sides of the car and filling it up. Murky liquid rushes and gushes right in her ears.

Soon the action is over and it's quiet again. The car, completely submerged, comes to a slow stop and the only movements are some silver bubbles skating across the ceiling of the vehicle before escaping to pop on the surface. Then it's just the dull pressure of the water pressing against her skin, and the terrible cold. Dark grey water; chilled mercury. Robin shudders.

"Don't say it," says de Villiers.

She snaps the lid off Blom's coffee and drinks in a deep mouthful.

Khaya frowns. "You okay?"

Her sneakers tap the table leg: five beats; ten. Fifteen—

"Just say it," says Devil.

"You just told me not to." Susman takes another big sip, desperate to get the warmth inside her, the liquid optimism.

"Let me guess. It's not just the transponder that's sitting at the bottom of that lake, is it?"

"I don't think so."

He curses in Afrikaans and shoves a pile of folders off his desk, and they land on the floor with a bang, reminding Susman of her earlier struggle with her suitcase. Her thumbnail bed is still tingling. De Villiers covers his eyes with this hands.

Robin downs what's left of Blom's coffee. Sometimes she feels she's in some kind of cruel stormy groundhog day, some gritty *deja vu* that threatens to suck her down into oblivion.

*Woman missing.*

*Woman found (dead).*

*Husband did it.*

"The husband did it?" ventures Khaya, as if he had been tuned into her mental tornado.

Susman glances at him sharply.

"Sorry," he says. "You always say—"

"No," says Susman. "Don't be sorry. You're probably right. It's just..." She puts down the paper cup and massages her temples.

*It's just that I'm sick to the pit of my stomach of men murdering women.*

16

. . .

She swallows hard, tries to keep herself together. She really shouldn't be here. "It just sometimes gets too much."

When Khaya blinks at her, his eyes are soft and full of regret.

Being a survivor of terrible violence carries with it so many heavy cloaks. One of which is that her colleagues often forget what she's been through and treat her like a regular person—which is Robin's preferred status quo—but then sometimes the memory hits them, mid-conversation, throbbing in the air between them, and they transform right there in front of her. In this case, from a lovely, young, cocky sergeant to a grey-skinned wretch.

"It's okay," says Susman.

Khaya searches her eyes. "It's not."

Susman looks away, avoiding the comment. It's ironic that sometimes it's the sensitivity of men that makes her come undone.

*How can you not hate men?* Khaya had asked her once.

*How do you know that I don't hate men?* she had replied.

Even if she wanted to, hating half the population is not a sustainable state of being. She doesn't have the energy for such a vast undertaking; she feels heavy enough as it is with all her cloaks on.

.   .   .

Devil's phone rings again. The floor is suddenly tidy; Susman hadn't seen him picking up the files.

"Ja," he says. "That's what we thought." He glances at Robin and crimps his lips; nods almost imperceptibly.

Susman chucks the stained paper cup into the bin and stands up, wiping the clamminess of her hands onto her jeans. "Ready to go?"

De Villiers grabs his jacket and car keys.

"Sithole," he says, and Khaya jumps to attention. "Text me the husband's address."

The drive to the South of Jo'burg is quiet; the car is crowded with contemplation. Now that Mixon is no longer missing, Robin knows she's free to go. She had agreed to stay to help find the woman, to save her life, but now all bets are off. She feels a strange loyalty to the victim; feels the need to reach for some kind of justice. So she allows Devil to shepherd her towards the first interview. She has, after all, already decided to stay for the day, and made the appropriate arrangements with the farm. She may as well make herself useful. Plus, he bought her NikNaks.

They pass a perspex factory, a stationery warehouse, Gold Reef City. Plastic, pencils and joy rides. Gold dust, pick axes, and shuttling, screaming, sugar-glazed children. Ribbons and cinnamon. It's another world; one that Robin will never be part of.

.   .   .

When they arrive at the Mixon residence there is a police car parked on the pavement. De Villiers and Susman shoot each other a relieved look. At least they won't have to break the news.

Joe Mixon paces across the scratched tiles, arms tightly folded across his stomach. De Villiers lifts his chin at the cop there and flashes his badge: a silver glint in the dim front passage. The cop nods; makes a quick introduction. He's happy to be let off the hook.

Mixon stops pacing and looks up at them, his brown skin smoky with denial and devastation.

"I need to see the body," he says, turning his wedding ring over and over on his finger.

"We'll arrange that," says Devil, and gets on his phone.

Robin takes in the simple, tasteful interior. A large mirror with a white mosaic frame, botanical-print cushions on the lounge suite, a duck-egg blue blanket thrown over the back of the three-seater couch. Susman imagines April Mixon standing in front of the mirror, imagines a flash of light (Camera flash? Lightning? Gunshot?) and Mixon's face changes from alive to dead.

Blush to blue.

Robin feels the lake water in her veins; hopes it will stop before it reaches her heart.

The scent of oranges draws her out of her reverie and makes her glance towards the large fruit bowl, crowned with a pineapple. She blinks once, twice. On the ivory glazed ceramic bottom she sees a gold wedding band hiding among the pink apples.

De Villiers ends the call and rejoins them.

Robin searches Joe's face. "Do you eat apples?" she asks.

Back at the station, Khaya has news for them.

"It's the Montclair station. Durban."

"Let me guess," says de Villiers. "They say it's their jurisdiction and we must bugger off."

Khaya shakes his head and laughs. "No. They're overworked and understaffed, just like us."

"Talking about understaffed, where the hell is Blom?"

"He'll be back tomorrow," says Khaya, and when Devil gives him a questioning look, he adds: "Maybe."

"What's the news?" asks Susman.

"There were a few rubberneckers at the lake this morning, right? I mean, it's not often that a car is driven into Lake Asha."

"Right."

"So one of them managed to get a shot of April Mixon after they retrieved her body. Montclair swears the area was cordoned off with emergency police tape, but—"

"But someone was able to grab a shot and he or she shared it anonymously on social media?" guesses Robin.

"Yes and no," says Khaya. "She wasn't bright enough to make it anonymous. And it's already been shared, like, a thousand times."

"Jackass," says Susman. Her mouth is dry. She searches in her handbag for a stick of chewing gum but comes up empty-handed. "Any link to the vic?"

"None found so far."

"She'll be cautioned for obstructing justice," says de Villiers.

"But here's the strange thing. She's actually helped us."

Susman and Devil both frown at Khaya. "How?"

"Listen to this. People in Glenmore are coming forward saying they recognise the dead woman in the picture, but that it's *not* April Mixon."

"What's that supposed to mean?" says de Villiers.

"Let me see the photo," says Susman.

Khaya hesitates. "Are you sure? There are no obvious injuries, but ... it's not pretty."

*Don't worry,* she's about to say. *I've seen worse in the mirror.*

He passes his phone to her.

The woman's face is marble. Robin zooms in to look at her hand; fingers sculpted from wax. She's wearing her wedding ring.


Susman calls Swift, the victim's place of work. She puts her phone on speaker, so the others can hear.

"Can I have the contact details of your Durban office?" Robin asks.

"We don't have a Durban office," says the receptionist.

"Your satellite office in Glenmore," says Susman. "Where Mrs Mixon used to commute to."

"Who told you that?" asks the woman.

"Her husband," says Robin. "He said she'd work one week here, one week there. Had been for years."

"It's true that she only came into the office every other week," says the woman. "It was some kind of flexitime arrangement. She used to work from home a lot."

*Joe Mixon said she was hardly ever home.*

"Believe me," the woman says, eager to hang up. "There is no Durban office."

Susman thanks the woman and ends the call.


Khaya stares at Robin with his mouth open. "Okay, I'm confused."

"If Blom was here, he'd say you were born confused," says de Villiers.

"And he'd be right," says Khaya.

Susan swings her legs up and lets her sneakers rest on a box of files. "You really need to clean this place up, Devil. What are these files, anyway?"

"Cold cases."

"Detective de Villiers likes to read them in his spare time."

"What spare time?" asks Robin.

Khaya snorts. "Exactly."

Robin can't imagine that Mrs Devil is very happy with that; choosing cold bodies over hers.

De Villiers sucks on the end of his pen. "So what the hell was April Mixon doing all that time in Durban?"

"Running a brothel? A casino? A dog-fight ring?"

"Nothing as exciting as that," says Khaya. He shows them a message on his phone.

*Montclair have confirmed that April Mixon was moonlighting at a different IT company in Glenmore. NOT Swift.*

"Corporate espionage?" ventures de Villiers. "Stealing the competition's secrets?"

"They're sending us details, including the residential address she supplied HR."

"I don't know about spying. I doubt someone would kill her for that, right? It's IT, for god's sake, not KGB."

Robin shifts in her chair.

*What was April Mixon hiding?*

"Either way, we can't investigate from here," says de Villiers. "Let's jump on a plane."

He starts clacking the keys on his keyboard. He types hard, with two fingers.

"I hate flying," says Susman.

"The flight is only an hour, max. And your bag is already packed."

"No way the Captain will approve the costs. Besides, Montclair seems to have it covered. We'd just be getting in the way."

"I've put it on my credit card," says Devil. "They'll reimburse me if we crack the case."

"I doubt it."

"*When* we crack the case," says Khaya.

Devil smacks his keyboard again and turns to Robin. "Flights confirmed. We've got twenty minutes to get to the airport."

When no one answers the door at the residential address in Durban, Devil springs the lock. In the old days Robin would have stopped, him, told him they'd have to wait for a warrant. Now she just feels a twinge of pride at how quickly and easily he breaks and enters.

The interior is brightly lit but stuffy. Susman opens a couple of windows. It's hard enough to breathe without being shut up in a dead woman's airless apartment.

De Villiers whistles. "Creepy," he says.

Robin looks in the direction of de Villiers' gaze. The mirror on the wall with the white mosaic frame is identical to the one in her Johannesburg home. So is the throw over the couch, and the botanical-print cushions. They walk through the flat. Same kettle, same toaster, same pyjamas bunched up under her pillow. Same toothbrush.

"Okay, things just got a little more interesting," says Susman. De Villiers walks over to her at the mantelpiece and inspects the picture in the brushed aluminium frame. A wedding photo.

"That's April," says Robin. "But that man is not Joe Mixon."

Robin's thoughts whirr and crack like a stuck fan.

"Same bride, same smile, same dress. Different groom."

De Villiers' phone rings; the caller ID says *Sgt Sithole*. He taps the screen twice. "You're on speakerphone."

"Hiya Boss," says Khaya. "I found something that ... may be nothing."

"It's never nothing," says Susman.

"I've been following those comments on Facebook. About that photo taken at the lake."

"Yes?"

"So, you know they're saying her name's not April Mixon?"

"I don't give a damn what Facebook says," yells Devil. "What does forensics say?"

"The DNA of the body matches the DNA on the razor you

brought in from Mixon's house. But get this: that DNA does not belong to April Mixon."

"How do we know this?"

"Because we have April Mixon's DNA on file."

"But the only way we'd have her profile on file is..."

"You guessed it, Boss."

Susman thinks out loud. "Because April Mixon was already dead."


Robin finds a drawer of white envelopes. Bills from the municipality, and her phone service provider, addressed to Tamara Wilson. Vet bills from a horse doctor, addressed to Mr Wilson, the man in the wedding photo.

A shadow of a ghost flits before Robin.

"Khaya, you still there?"

"I'm here."

"See what you can find on this person. Got a pen?"

There is a shuffling as Khaya searches, then he's back. "Shoot."

"Tamara Wilson."

"Hang on," says the sergeant. "That's on my list already. From the Facebook comments. Some people knew her as Tamara Wilson."

"Get hold of those commenters," says Devil. "We'll need statements from them."

. . .

26

"Who are you?" says a male voice, making them both jump, and de Villiers automatically reaches for his gun. Robin's fingers play on her denim hip; she didn't bring hers.

"Whoah!" he says, when he sees Devil's Z88. He puts up his hands. "What's going on?"

"Mr Wilson?" asks Susman.

"Who's asking?"

De Villiers flashes his detective badge with his left hand. His right hand is steadily aimed at Wilson's chest. Something changes in the man's face when he sees the silver shield. Robin thinks he might faint, but then he jettisons out of the apartment.


"Hey!" shouts de Villiers. He holsters his gun and gives chase. Out the front door, left to the emergency stairs, their feet beating the chafed concrete as they sprint.

Robin calls for back-up, but she knows that chances of them arriving in time—or at all—are slim. She hears a gunshot and her adrenaline spikes. She runs to the balcony; from where she's standing, three storeys up, she sees Wilson round a corner and jump a fence and then catch his breath behind the cover of a wheelie bin. De Villiers can't see where he went and keeps running.

"Fence!" she yells at him and gestures wildly. "Fence!"

He gets the message, u-turns, and heaves himself up over the shaking wire. Wilson hears him land on the other side and peels off again, but not fast enough. De Villiers launches himself at the man and brings him down, hard, smashing his teeth on the tarmac.

De Villiers hauls him up and handcuffs him, breathing hard and pushing the man forward with unsympathetic hands while Wilson dribbles blood onto the front of his white collared shirt. A police car arrives, siren blaring, tyres squealing, and out jump two cops with semi-automatic pistols in their hands.

"You shouldn't have run," says Susman to Wilson, who is holding a wet cloth to his mouth. The interrogation room is a slab of chilled air. The metal table leaches all the warmth from Robin's arms, and she rubs them to get rid of the numbness she feels.

"We didn't even suspect you," says de Villiers, "until you started running."

"I panicked." Wilson's lips are swollen, his jaw is bruised blue.

"You saved us a week of investigation."

"We didn't even know you existed until you showed up in that wedding photo," says Robin.

Wilson's eyes flutter closed.

"Do you want to tell us about that photo?"

"No," he says. "No. I don't."

"You misunderstand," says Devil. "It wasn't a request."

"I'm not saying anything till my lawyer arrives."

Robin laughs. "You've been watching too much TV."

De Villiers shows Robin the screen of his phone. It's a message from Khaya.

*TOX REPORT: Trace ketamine found in vic's blood.*

Robin knows ketamine. She closes her eyes and breathes in the memory-scent of the storeroom at the farm. Lawn fertiliser, pesticide sprays; veterinary drugs. They use Ketalar to tranquillise the sheep.

She remembers the white envelopes she found in the drawer in the Wilson flat. "You ride horses," says Robin, but he ignores her.

She raises her voice so that he'll look at her. "How does it feel?" she asks.

Wilson drags his eyes up to hers, and she counters his gaze.

"How does it feel to find out that your wife was leading a double life?"

He shrugs. It's not news to him. Not anymore, anyway.

"Must have made you angry," says de Villiers. "When you found out."

"An entirely separate existence. A job you knew nothing about. Friends you've never met."

Wilson looks away, ignoring them.

"Two lives. Two wedding rings. Two husbands."

She pictures the twin kettles, the twin toasters. The mirrors reflecting each other over and over again so that you fell you're falling backwards into an Escher painting.

"She was lying to you. Lying to everyone, actually. She fooled you for years. That must have made you want to teach her a lesson. Right?"

Face of stone.

"Do you know that she bought the exact same kettle and toaster for her other house? The *exact same kettle*."

"And those pillows," says de Villiers. "That blanket."

The stone splits; crumbles. Wilson, elbows on the table, forces his palms together, then drops his face into them.

"Bringing up the kettle was a stroke of genius," says de Villiers on the plane back to Johannesburg.

"Was it?" says Robin. "I was just making conversation. You're the one who caught him."

She feels almost cheerful.

"I haven't seen you smile in a long time," he says.

"Catching wife-killers has that effect on me."

"It's like he expected the other questions, you know. Expected to be asked about her job and her car and her murder. Probably had rehearsed responses for those. But there's something about a kettle. About the real, everyday things they shared. He wasn't expecting that—being equated to a kitchen appliance—it's not good for a man's ego. It cracked him in half; I saw it happen. A full confession within an hour of bringing him in. That must be a record, even for you."

"I haven't heard you talk so much in a long time," teases Robin, and de Villiers catches himself laughing.

But then his smile disappears. "You're so damn good at this job."

"Don't start," she says. "I'm not staying."

"Okay," Devil says. He sits back in his chair and sighs in surrender. "Okay."

## 3
## THE SHELTER

THE DANK AIR that presses up against Anna's cheeks is cool and thick—coffin air—as if the soil that keeps the Shelter buried is closing in on them, pushing at the walls, ready to crack bones and smother lips and noses. Anna reminds herself to breathe.

They shuffle along the narrow passage, their slippers shining the concrete floor. The susurration is a moth beating its velvet wings in Anna's ears: shuffle, shuffle, shuffle.

She's looking for Simon, but all the Dwellers look the same from the back, covered head to toe in coarse brown hooded robes aged with grime and black. Underneath the robes are old pyjamas and cast-offs. The Dwellers don't wash their clothes; there is not enough water down here for such luxuries.

"Simon," she whispers, but he doesn't turn around. "Simon!"

"Shhh!" hisses Anthony, frowning at her, his elbow hard against hers.

"Bugger off, Tony," she says.

"We are on our way to the Sanctum," he says, straightening his hood. "There should be silence."

"Keep your mouth shut, then," she says.

He turns, ready to scold her. "Anna."

William turns around, his irises black petals in the dim light; his pale, lined face pulled tight with annoyance. "Anthony," he says. "Please respect the sacred rites of the Crossing Ceremony. Silence to the Sanctum."

Anthony's mouth opens. Anna thinks how much she despises his thick lips, his downy facial hair. Wishes that it was his turn to cross, instead of Peter, who at least has interesting things to tell her of Outside, and a sharp sense of humour.

"I was just—" argues Anthony.

"Tony." William's jaws are clenched.

Anthony pauses, and Anna sees the vein running over his temple like a snake.

How Anna hates that pulsating blood serpent. She moves ahead, ignoring the daggers in his eyes.

"Yes, sir." Anthony adjusts his hood again, and shuffles forward.


They reach the candlelit Sanctum, scented with soil, matches and hot wax. Anna spots Simon and manoeuvres herself to his side. She glances around, then surreptitiously takes his warm hand in hers, which makes him jump.

"I need to speak to you," she whispers.

"Are you okay?" he asks. "It looks like you've been crying."

"I need to tell you something. After the ceremony. It's important."

"What? Tell me now!"

"I can't," she whispers. "It's—"

"Shhh!" says Anthony.

William clears his throat and raises himself to his full height. "We'll have silence in the Sanctum."


The room hushes. Anna looks around at the familiar faces, glowing like moonstones from within the dark recesses of their hoods. They stand in silence, listening out for the Matriarch. Anna's heart is beating louder than usual. Loud enough for her to think that Anthony will hear it and tell her to keep quiet. Soon enough, a pair of high-heeled shoes strut down the passage, towards them, and Simon lets go of Anna's hand.


Adira enters and smiles, opening her arms wide as if to hug them all. They smile back at her with flames in their eyes.

"Thank you, William," she speaks just loudly enough to be heard. "Good evening, fellow Dwellers."

Adira click-clacks over the cold floor and sits down in the only chair in the room. She takes a breath and looks over the people gathered in the Sanctum, making eye contact and smiling reassuringly at the more anxious faces.

"We are here," Adira says, "to witness the most sacred of Shelter rites: The Crossing Ceremony."

There is a collective intake of breath. The emotion in the room wraps around Anna and threatens to stifle her. Her lungs balloon.

"While it may be difficult to say goodbye to our dear friend Peter," says Adira, "we respect and revere his most selfless decision to take the noose around his neck."

There is a stifled sob from the back of the room; Anna swallows her own cry.

"Those of us he leaves behind should not be sad, but rejoice in his decision." Adira's voice is melodic, calming, beautiful: a crystal mountain stream. "Peter's brave last act will bring us more days of nourishment in our famine. It is the Ultimate Sacrifice. We must keep in our hearts the knowledge that he dies so that we may live."

Gasps of grief; unwelcome tears. Anna avoids the pained expressions of the others. Instead she stares at the Matriarch's red high heels while her heart aches.

"And by this sacrifice Peter will obtain that which none of us left behind have," says Adira. "Today, this hour, he will cross over to a better place. Death brings with it the ultimate freedom."

"Peter," she says. "Are you ready?"

The crowd peels away to make space for Peter as he emerges from the monastery of brown robes. He nods at Adira.

"Please hand me your key."

Peter takes the loop of twine from around his neck and holds it up. The silver key glints in the soft light. Instinctively, Anna reaches for her own key and presses her fingertips against it.

"Anna," says the Matriarch, startling her. "Please take Peter's key and hang it on the wall along with those of the others who have Crossed. It is in hallowed company."

Anna's heart is clamouring again. She makes her way through the gathering and takes Peter's key from him. He puts a reassuring palm on her shoulder. She kisses his hand, then hangs the key on a newly-hammered nail in the wall.

"William," says Adira, standing up. "Simon. Please help Peter onto the chair."

The men take Adira's chair and place it in the middle of the room. They help a trembling Peter to step up onto the seat.

"Peter," Adira says. "Your gift to us is valued beyond measure. Do you have anything to say?"

Peter starts talking, but his voice is thick. He takes a moment to compose himself. "Is there anything to say?" he asks.

"Only you know the answer to that, dear friend."

"I've said everything," Peter replies. "I'm ready."

"Then let us pray," says Adira. "Everyone, hold your keys."

The Dwellers grasp their silver and chant the well-known prayer together.

· · ·

"Our Father Cramer, to whom we owe our lives. Come fire, come storm, may God keep you safe, as you keep us safe. Come disease, come suffering, may you be as sheltered as we are, in this holy space you have provided for us. Amen."

"And so the key is replaced by the noose," Adira says, nodding at Peter, who adjusts his feet on the chair and, with shaking hands, puts the rope around his neck.

"Cramer knows and appreciates what you are doing, as we all do. Feel the love around you; you are surrounded by joyous affection."

Peter swallows hard and blinks away his tears.

Adira stands before him. "May God be with you."

The Dwellers echo her. "May God be with you," they chant.

"Go now, in peace."

Peter steps off the chair, inadvertently kicking the back and knocking it over. It clatters loudly on the hard floor. The people flinch and turn away from Peter's convulsing body, and then it is over.

Caron, the youngest Dweller, sobs out loud.

"Thank you all," says the Matriarch. "Dismissed."

They shuffle out of the Sanctum, back down the passage, and into the adjoining rooms, chatting softly in small groups.

Caron can no longer hold back her grief and sobs loudly into her hands. Her shoulders heave with the pent-up emotion.

"Caron," says William sharply. "That's enough."

Caron straightens up, tries to stop crying. "Sorry, father. I'm just so... It's just so sad."

"You disappoint me," says William. "You should know that a Crossing is not to be mourned. Indeed, the opposite! Peter has given us a great gift."

"Yes, Father. A great gift."

"Can I trust you now to be sensible?"

"Sensible?"

"No more tears," says William.

Caron sniffs. "I'll try."

"Caron," he says, anger barbing his words. "I said *no more tears.*"

He pats her roughly on the back and stalks away.


Anna can't stand it; Caron's just a child, after all. She draws the weeping girl into a hug.

"Father said not to be sad, but I can't help it."

"Of course you're sad," says Anna. "Peter was wonderful. It won't be the same in the Shelter without him. I spent the whole morning trying to talk him out of handing in his key, but he had made up his mind. He wanted to do the honourable thing."

"Oh, I hate Crossings. I know we're supposed to celebrate them but ... I can't even bear to look at his key on that wall."

"Caron!" scolds William, seemingly appearing out of nowhere, and making them both flinch. "Go to the sleeping quarters until you have your emotions under control."

"William, please," says Anna. "Her tears are natural, and not offending anyone."

William's eyes pop. "I'll ask you not to interfere with our family discipline."

"Are we not all one family?" she asks.

His face glows with fury.

Anna turns to the young girl. "Caron, would you mind feeding Chairman Miaow? He was last on my bed."

Grateful for the excuse, Caron scampers.


Bristling, William approaches Adira as she stands, looking at the keys on the wall, while two Dwellers take Peter's limp body from the noose.

She looks at him and sighs. "Ah, hello, William. I was expecting you."

"A word, please, Adira."

"That's exactly what I was expecting."

"I have a few things to say."

"Of course you do."

"What's that supposed to mean?"

"Mean? It doesn't mean anything."

"I know you think I'm overly strict with the Dwellers, but if I don't do it, who will?"

"They are not sheep, William. They do not need to be shepherded."

"I disagree."

"Of course you do. You want to be the shepherd."

"Only because you are too lenient with them."

"You speak about them as if they are children. We haven't had a child in the shelter since your daughter grew up."

William knots his hands into fists. "I just think that the discipline is waning."

"According to you, the discipline has been waning for the last twenty years. I—still--don't see a problem. Now, is there something specific you'd like to talk about?"

"Yes," he takes a deep breath. "First of all, I don't mean to disrespect your position as Matriarch, but—"

"Ha. There's always a 'but'."

"Do you really think those shoes are appropriate for a Crossing Ceremony?"

"These shoes? Why wouldn't they be? Because they're red? Or because they have heels?"

"Everyone else wears slippers, as they should."

"I wasn't aware there was a rule governing appropriate footwear."

"Slippers are comfortable, modest, and quiet to walk in. They should be the requisite footwear in the Shelter."

"William. I am not about to tell the Dwellers what they should and shouldn't wear. As it is, no one gets to choose—to really choose—their clothes. They just arrive in smelly boxes!"

"Those clothes are gifts from Cramer!"

"I know! It doesn't make them any less smelly. Just like it doesn't make the bread he gives us any less stale. The point is that I will not start to take away the Dweller's small freedoms when their *actual* freedom is denied them."

"That's the other thing. Your language!"

"My language?"

"You, blatantly using the F-word. And in the Crossing Ceremony no less!"

"I'm thinking of changing that rule. The concept of freedom—"

William's horror is clear. "Adira! Please!"

"The concept of the *F-word* is alive and well in everyone's heads —not being allowed to say the word out loud doesn't change that fact."

"The way you're going ... you mean to destroy all the rules of the Shelter!"

"The Shelter is a living organism. It will evolve organically as other natural things do, according to what is best for its people. It is not a crowd that needs to be fenced in by petty rules."

Adira looks around at the concrete walls.

"After all, we are jailed enough by these ever-present concrete walls."

William frowns at her. "This 'jail' is the only thing keeping us alive!"

"Yes, William, and we need to keep our spirits alive, too. That's why I wear these shoes. That might seem vain or silly to you, but they're the most beautiful things I have down here, and I —*we*—all need a way to keep happy. Or, at the very least, sane. Look at what happened to Peter."

They both glance over at Peter's still body, lying on the make-shift stretcher and covered with a dirty shroud.

"Peter chose to cross over. He sacrificed himself for us."

"He was also depressed, and needed a way out."

"I can't believe what I'm hearing. It's like you're laying aside all your Shelter values. It's worrying, Adira, I must say. It's ... it's extremely worrying."

Adira pauses, and her eyes cloud over. "Perhaps I have started wondering..."

She shakes her head, changing her mind about sharing. "Nothing. You're right, it's important to preserve the harmony we have established in the Shelter. Let's continue this conversation another time. I need to see Anthony urgently about the—"

William grabs her elbow. "Wait, there's something else."

Adira shakes his hand loose. "Can it wait?"

"I don't believe so."

"It's about Anna," he says, his skin still hot from their earlier exchange. "She's been stepping out of line."

43

"You *do* realise you're not Anna's father?"

"Perhaps that's the problem. She doesn't have a father figure to teach her right from wrong."

"That doesn't qualify you for the role. It is none of my business how strict you are with Caron and Michael but that approach simply won't work with Anna. Apart from that, she's an adult. She's twenty years old!"

"She's defiant."

"She's an independent, spirited woman ... who has lived in a basement her entire life."

"I've heard her speaking about Outside with the others. I've heard her say the F-word."

"Of course she's going to talk about freedom. It's her biggest desire. You can't talk someone out of that."

"I've even heard that she was singing!"

"Good God, William, not *singing!*"

"You can make fun of me, Adira, but singing is against the Shelter rules. No unnecessary noise."

"*Noise?* Is her singing voice that bad?"

"You can joke, but the rules exist for a reason."

"They do."

"They keep us safe. They keep us alive."

"Yes. But I don't believe that after living here for twenty years it will be Anna's bad singing that gives us away. I'm sure she wasn't belting out show-tunes, or we all would have heard her."

Adira begins walking away, but William reaches for her again.

"I caught her and Simon in the North wing, unchaperoned."

"What?"

"It was before dinner last night. I went to fetch my scarf and they ... well, they ... sprung apart."

"Are you ... sure?"

"Absolutely sure. I was going to say something there and then but they both just greeted me and left the room before I had the chance to voice my—"

"Well. I suppose it was bound to happen. Anyone can see they've been in love for years."

"But the *rules*—"

"Yes, William. The rules, the rules."

"No procreation!"

"A rule that you happened to break twice during your stay here."

"For God's sake, Bet and I are a married couple."

"The rule is *no babies*, William. Wedlock has nothing to do with it. Noise and hunger are the only reason that babies are not allowed."

"You should speak to Anna. She doesn't listen to me. If anything, she does the opposite of what I ask. She needs to know the gravitas of the situation. Can I trust you to make it clear to her?"

Anna catches up to Simon in the passage.

"There you are," he says, and smiles.

"Come with me now," she whispers, "to the East room."

"Unchaperoned?"

Anna laughs, but the sound has an edge of desperation to it.

"Are you okay? You look pale. You're not yourself."

"I've just watched a man I've known all my life die right in front of me. Of course I'm not okay. How can *you* be okay?"

"I'm strengthened by the sacrifice Peter made, as I have been by previous Crossings."

Anna sighs impatiently. "Are you coming?"

"Do we need to be alone? Can't we just talk in the West Room?"

"What now? Are you scared of being alone with me?" She moves her mouth towards his ear and speaks in a low voice. "Scared of what I might do to you?"

"Stop," Simon says, looking around. "Someone might be listening."

"Come, then. You're right to be scared. I want you all to myself."

"Anna." It's meant as a gentle rebuke, but the desire in his eyes burns bright.

"I want your lips, your hands. I want to feel your hands on me."


Anthony's face appears like a mask on the wall. "Simon."

"Jesus, Tony, I hate it when you sneak up on us like that."

"Yes?" says Simon, blushing.

"I need your meal plan for next week."

"Can it wait? We're in the middle of something here."

Anthony stands his ground. "It should have been in yesterday."

"It can wait," says Anna.

"Actually, no, I don't think it can."

Anna grinds her teeth. "Really, Tony? You think the Shelter is going to crumble if we don't know exactly which tins of food we're going to be opening in the next few days, and in which order?" She looks at Simon for support, but he avoids her eyes.

"Tony's right. I should do the meal plan now. It's a day late."

Anna narrows her eyes at them, then gives up, and storms off.

"I thought I might find you here," says Adira. She sits on Anna's bed, and can feel the broken bedsprings. "It's good to see you resting."

"Given my 'delicate condition'?" says Anna. She puts down her knitting.

Adira laughs. "Yes. How are you feeling?"

"Sad. Angry. Desperate to get out of here."

"I meant physically. Do you think everything is progressing well with the pregnancy?"

"I don't know. I guess so. But I don't know anything about pregnancy, apart from what I've read in that old book you found for me."

"A doctor should be looking after you."

"Mythical creatures, doctors. Do you think there are any left in the world Outside?"

"Perhaps, but certainly not in South Africa. Or whatever South Africa has become."

"But surely the Marauders need doctors?"

"I don't think the Marauders thought they needed anything. Cramer says it's nothing but burned land, now."

"I know I've never been Outside but it infuriates me to think of the waste. I can't believe some of the things I read. Things like art and apple farms and cinemas. It's difficult for me to imagine they are real, and not some writer's fantasy."

"They were real, once upon a time. They don't exist anymore."

Anna imagines the scorched earth, the dead animals; burnt out cars and bitter smoke. And the terrifying Marauders: violent pirates ravaging everything in their path.

"And to think we are the lucky ones."

"I know it's difficult to believe that sometimes."


"I tried to talk Peter out of it, you know," says Anna. "Handing in his key. I know that it goes against the Shelter's values but I didn't care about how much trouble I would get into, as long as he stayed alive."

"Sweet Anna, you have no idea how much trouble you are in, with or without your chats with Peter."

"I know. It makes me feel sick. Every morning I wake up and think it was all a bad dream, this pregnancy, but then I reach down and there's this thickening; this bump. And the nausea—a constant reminder that I have betrayed everyone in the Shelter."

"Don't get upset, my dear. No good will come of it. There's no un-spilling the milk."

"And you, being so forgiving. How can you? Don't you see that this extra mouth to feed nullifies Peter's sacrifice?"

Anna's eyes fill up with tears.

"Peter had had enough of living down here. It was not the life for him. He no longer had hope, and he said that is the one thing he couldn't live without."

"But hope for what?"

"It's difficult for you to understand—you've never lived Outside —but there are certain things that you wouldn't want to live without, if you knew about them. You youngsters are in a far better position than us—you have less to long for."


Adira looks at the wall Anna's bed is pushed up against. Old pictures of forests and volcanoes, a grizzly bear; vanilla ice-cream. A snow-capped mountain.

"I long for a thousand things," Anna says. "I long for fresh air and sunshine and to feel a tree's bark and to walk barefoot on grass. I long to swim in the ocean..."

Adira smiles. "We never did reach a consensus if the Shelter Dwellers should be allowed to read books."

Anna's eyes are stretched wide. "Without books I would surely die."

"At least they allow us *some* freedoms, even if it's all in our heads. Perhaps a swim in the sea in a book is better than no swim in the sea at all."

"Or, in my case," says Anna, "not even knowing that an astonishing thing like an ocean exists."

Adira grazes Anna's knee with her hand. "Does Simon know?"

"About the ocean?"

"About the baby."

"Not yet."

Adira purses her lips. "Anna."

"I keep trying to tell him, but ... privacy."

"Hard to come by."

"Yes. Especially with William always looming. And Tony constantly sneaking up on me."

"William told me about seeing you and Simon 'unchaperoned'."

"Mortifying."

"Don't worry about it. And try not to worry too much about the baby."

Anna fidgets with the scrappy teddy bear on her bed. "'The Baby'. I can't believe this is real. There is going to be *a baby*."

"Are you scared?"

"Petrified."

"You know, up there, on the Outside, before The Great War, a baby was usually seen as a good thing. A blessing. A gift from God."

"I can't imagine that," says Anna, holding the old toy against her belly. "If fire wasn't against the rules I'd worry that I'd be burned at the stake."

"That means we did a good job brainwashing you youngsters."

Anna laughs, and then stops suddenly. "Clearly not good enough."

∼

"Here's my meal plan for the week," says Simon, handing William a scrap of paper. "I've just been doing stock-take of the larder. It's bad news, I'm afraid."

William takes the list without looking up; he's busy making notes in his ledger. "It's late. You were supposed to hand it in yesterday."

"I told him," says Anthony.

"Did you hear what I said?" asks Simon. "It's bad news. Very bad news."

William stops, puts his pen down on the table. "Okay, let's go through it."

The younger men sit down at the table with him.

"I can see why Peter hated this job," says Simon. "Even on a really tight menu—a starvation ration—we only have enough food in the larder for a few more weeks. We ran out of fresh food 2 weeks ago. Cramer hasn't Come Down for almost a month now—we still have some dry supplies, tinned food and preserves—"

"I see," says William.

"And Peter's Crossing?" asks Anthony. "It must have helped."

"Yes, of course, but we still have 21 mouths to feed. If we really, really stretch it—and I'm talking about everyone going hungry—we can maybe make a month, 6 weeks."

"I see we'll be eating maize at every meal." Anthony pulls a weary face. "Maize meal or powdered potatoes."

"Tony," scolds William. "You should be grateful that we have anything at all. Do you have any idea how difficult it is for Cramer to find food Outside? Do you realise the danger he puts himself in every time he tends his secret garden? Every time he puts together a supplies parcel for us?"

Anthony doesn't reply; his mouth is a hard line.

"Do you think..." says Simon. "Do you think that's why he hasn't Come Down? Because something has happened to him?"

William's face is dark with worry. "I don't know."

"He's never left us for this long before," says Anthony. "I think there must be something wrong."

"I thought he was looking particularly old on his last visit," says Simon. "I'm sure he's ill. Or maybe there is simply no more food left. The Marauders have taken it all. We knew that day would come."

"Or maybe he's run out of currency?" says Anthony.

William angles his head. "He shouldn't have. We gave him 22 blankets last time. That should have been enough for a couple of months of supplies." He taps the table with his fingers, then takes up his pen again, opens his ledger. "But there's no point in ruminating. All we can do is make sure we use the supplies as sparingly and responsibly as possible."

Simon nods. "And pray that Cramer Comes Down."

Caron's cheeks are flushed with emotion and wonder. "So ... are you saying that those creatures are real?"

Anna laughs. "Of course they are!"

"They can't be," she says.

"They are."

"I'm so glad we live down here. I'd hate to live with those things."

"Oh, don't be such a wimp. It's not like they're roaming the streets. They're in the wild. Or, at least, they used to be. Who knows what exists now and what doesn't. Hyenas might be extinct altogether."

"Good!" says Caron. "They're frightful."

"Nonsense," says Anna. "Hyenas are beautiful."

"Now, that's going too far," says Simon.

Caron giggles. "Hello, Simon."

"What's the lesson today, lovely Anna?"

Anna closes the tattered magazine to show him the cover. "National Geographic. It's over thirty years old, and half of the pages have fallen out, but some of the pictures are still lovely."

"Anna's teaching me biology. About wild animals. Did you know that crocodiles have been around for over two hundred million years? Or that giraffes' tongues are blue?"

"I did not."

"Well, it's true. I can't imagine it, but it's true."

"When the only animal you've known your whole life is a little cat, it's not surprising that the other animals seem ... outrageous."

"Next you'll be teaching Caron about Plato's cat."

"Who's Plato?" asks Caron.

"Didn't you know, Caron, that Chairman Miaow is not really a cat. He is merely a—old and grumpy—copy of the original idea of a cat?"

"I have no idea what you just said."

"I sense a huge gap in your education. Anna, you've got lots of work to do in the philosophy department."

"Rubbish!" says Anna. "Philosophy can wait till she's eighteen. This stuff is much more fun."

"Your blankets are coming along nicely. I haven't knitted in a while."

"I think it's the hunger that motivates us. We already have 6 to give Cramer. They're piling up. Do you know if there is any news?"

Simon clears his throat. "Shall we walk?"

"You're teaching her about Outside?" whispers Simon, holding her shoulder.

"Yes. Why not?" His hand feels good on her shoulder. It makes her want to peel off her robe so she can feel his warm skin against hers.

"You know very well *why not*."

"Argh. I know. William. The rules."

"Yes. The rules. There's a reason why we're not supposed to speak about Outside."

"I know ... but I'm starting to think it's a stupid rule."

"Still."

"And I'm sick of stupid rules. In fact, I'd like to show you how sick I am of them. Shall we check if the North room is free?"

Simon hesitates. "Does that mean what I think it means?"

Anna blinks at him. "Only if you have a particularly dirty imagination."

"Anna ... I don't know what's gotten into you..."

"But you like it," she says, and takes his hand.

Simon looks from side to side. "I..."

"Yes, yes, you shouldn't, but you do."

"I just think we should—"

"Ah, there's no one here. Quick, kiss me, before anyone comes."

They kiss. Tentatively at first, then deeper as everything else fades away.

Simon sighs. "You don't know what you're doing to me."

"Tell me."

He kisses her again, then pulls away. "Oh, God. I can't do this."

"Of course you can."

"*We* can't do this. It's too risky."

"I don't care anymore."

"If you knew—"

"What? That there's no more food? Everyone knows that."

"Then you know we can't take the risk."

"What if I told you it was too late?"

"You don't know that. Cramer may still Come Down."

"I mean too late. Too late."

"What?"

"Give me your hand."

"I don't think we should—"

"Shut up and give me your hand."

Anna takes Simon's hand and puts it on her swollen abdomen.

"What?"

"Can you feel it?"

"Your stomach? Yes, I can feel it."

"And that?"

As the knowledge hits Simon he reclaims his hand and raises it to his mouth. "Wait. Wait."

"Wait? I've been waiting all my life."

His face is white wax. "For this?"

"Yes. For this. For what we have. For *something*. Don't you see? *Something had to happen.*"

He shakes his head. "We're in so much trouble."

"Can't you think of something else to say?

"God, Anna," he says, pulling his hair. "I want to say that I'm happy. That I'd love to have a baby with you. And while that's all true, none of it matters."

"Of course it matters," she says, eyes desperately seeking the reaction she needs. "It's all that matters."

"You're wrong. I wish you were right, but you're wrong. There's no more food. That baby won't be one more mouth to feed, it'll be one more person to starve to death."

"But we'll have enough food till Cramer Comes Down again. We always do. We always worry but then he always Comes Down."

"We'll have silence in the Sanctum," says William.

The Dwellers stand in a hushed silence. Candlelight paints the walls.

The high-heels clack, and Adira appears.

"Thank you, William. Good evening, fellow Dwellers."

The smell of fear and unwashed clothes is ripe. The gathering whisper their quiet greeting.

Adira takes a breath. "This is the trial of Anna Fourie and Simon Van Zyl. As this is a trial, the floor is open to respectful commentary, so the rule of silence in the Sanctum is momentarily void."

There is a quiet murmuring and shushing.

"Anna and Simon are charged with breaking the all-important rule, that of 'No Procreation'. How do you plead?

"As you can see, Matriarch, it is true that I am expecting a child."

"Guilty, then," says William.

"Yes, guilty. As you were too, I believe, with both your son and daughter."

The Dwellers raise their eyebrows and nod. Her words are true.

William is furious. "How dare you?"

"Perhaps we'll stop at making the mistake once, when others clearly didn't."

"Harlot!" says Anthony, glowering from the corner.

Simon turns to him. "Tony, did you call William's wife the same thing on hearing *her* news?"

"That's enough," says Adira. "Respectful commentary is all that is allowed here tonight."

"They have broken the all-important rule," spits Anthony. "They have put all our lives at risk. They should be punished."

Anna gasps and holds her stomach. The Dwellers around her move closer, hold her arms, support her.

"Anna?" says Adira. "Are you in pain?"

Anna pants. "Yes, Matriarch. Thank you. I have been in some discomfort today. It comes and goes. Please, let's continue."

"We admit we have broken the rule, and broken your trust," says Simon. "To all the Dwellers: we are incredibly sorry that this has happened. I know we are all hungry. We've been hungry for weeks. And why should you share your ration because we have made a mistake? That is why I am relinquishing my share to the baby, when the time comes.

"Relinquishing your share?"

"Yes, Matriarch. The child will have my ration."

"And what will you eat?"

"I will do well on water, until Cramer Comes Down again."

"It's not just the food that's the problem," says Anthony. "Babies aren't allowed because they make so much noise. A screaming baby will be like a siren to the Marauders. They'll find us all and kill us!"

The gathering flinches.

"You all remember what Cramer said the last time he was here," says Anthony. "He said the Marauders are getting so hungry that they—"

"That's enough!" says Adira.

"They'll find us! Imagine what they'd do to that baby!"

"Anthony, that's enough."

Adira waits for them to quieten down. "The noise level of an infant *is* a concern. And it needs to be addressed. But this is not the forum. Nor is this the forum for scaremongering."

"You can't hide the truth from us," says Anthony. "Cramer tells us the truth!"

"Tony, leave the Sanctum."

"No!"

"Tony!"

"No, I will not leave. I will not be silenced in this way."

"Leave or you will be escorted."

"I will have my say."

Adira bangs on the side of her chair. "Then say what you need to say."

"The punishment I put forward for Anna and Simon is a forced Crossing."

Gasps of horror ripple over the crowd.

Adira pauses. "A forced Crossing? There is no such thing. A Crossing is a voluntary act of bravery and sacrifice."

"A forced Crossing is what they deserve. It would simply be

giving Anna what she's always wanted. Freedom, freedom, freedom, she never shuts up about it! Well, let her have it!"

Adira frowns at Anthony. "You'd kill a mother and her infant?"

"If it would save others."

"But if we sentenced them to death, how would we be any different to the Marauders?"

"The child is illegitimate!"

"What do you know of legitimacy?" asks Simon.

"It is illegitimate by its very existence."

Anna doubles over. "Oh!"

Anthony yells in frustration "What?"

"Anna? Anna?" says Simon. "What is it?"

Anna moans. "It's happening. It's too soon."

Simon catches her as she collapses.

"I've never seen anything so beautiful," says Anna. Her voice is strained and weak.

"She is indeed beautiful," says Adira.

"Precious little thing," says Caron. "Like a doll."

Simon looks down at the bundle in his arms. "She's so tiny. She weighs nothing."

"Well done, you two," says Adira. "You were both very brave."

"And you!" says Anna to Adira. "Delivering a baby of all things. Who would have guessed?"

Adira laughs. "Certainly not me!"

The baby starts to fuss, straining for food.

"I think she's hungry again," says Simon.

"How can she possibly be hungry again?"

Simon hands her to Anna, who puts the baby to her breast.

"She has a good appetite," says Adira. "It's good."

Her words are like grey smoke in the air.

Anna starts to say something, but Adira interrupts her. "Shush, dear, it's good. Just as this moment is good. Let's worry about everything else another day."

Adira's waiting for them at the table in the West Room. Simon and William arrive with heavy footsteps, as if their slippers have turned into shuffling slabs of soft lead. Adira gestures for them to sit down.

"All right," she says, crossing her arms to keep warm, knowing their words will chill her. "This is the meeting we never wanted to have."

Simon puts on a brave face. "I think we need to start preparing for the Ending."

William recoils. "There's still a chance that Cramer will Come Down."

"Yes," says Simon. "But it becomes more remote by the day."

"Cramer would not forsake us," says William.

"No, he wouldn't. But nor could he live forever. It's a wonder he has survived this long."

"He has his ways. He has a small measure of protection."

"Not from disease. Or age."

Adira exhales as if she's been holding her breath. "It must wear down a man to be responsible for so many lives. Especially in those abhorrent conditions out there."

"He hasn't been down in over six weeks now. I think we need to … to do what needs to be done."

"Surely we can wait just a few more weeks," says William.

"There is nothing left," says Simon. "Even the rats are dying. Chairman Miaow will be next."

"All right," says Adira, straightening her spine. "It looks like we have no choice. We'll start preparations for the Ending tomorrow."

They sit in silence for a moment.

"I can't believe it's finally happening," says Simon. "Baby Bella —she's only a few weeks old."

William puts his hand on the younger man's shoulder, and gains some strength from the gesture. "We knew the day would come, son. Let us be courageous."

Adira and William walk into the Sanctum together.

Caron jumps. "Is it true?" she asks with saucer-eyes. "Is it true what they've been saying?" Her hair is untidy, her skin flickers with an anxious sheen.

The Dwellers are agitated. They talk amongst themselves in worried whispers, and it sounds as if there is a plague of locusts in the room.

"It is with a heavy heart—" says Adira, and the people stop to listen. The hungry locusts vanish. "It is with a heavy heart that I stand here before you tonight and tell you that our story is over —will be over—tomorrow afternoon. We are currently preparing for the Ending."

Gasps and moans of shock perforate the silence. Baby Bella fusses, and Anna holds her tight to her breast, placing her little finger in the baby's mouth to pacify her.

Adira raises her voice. "I know. I know it's difficult to—"

"Settle down, please," says William. "Keep it down. Don't make this more difficult than it has to be."

Anthony's eyes spark with anger. "Do we not get a say?"

"Of course you do," says Adira. "But unfortunately nothing you say can change this outcome. The larder is all but bare, and we have no reason to believe that Cramer will Come Down again. All stories have their endings—it is natural and good—and now we have ours."

"Cramer has forsaken us!" cries Anthony.

William takes a step towards Anthony. "Cramer did everything he could to keep us alive. Two decades of scrounging for food and supplies. Twenty years of putting himself in danger, keeping us a secret from the evil Outside."

Simon clears his throat. "Will you take us through the rites? What will happen tomorrow?"

"How do we then Cross?" asks Anna. "There are too many people to take the noose around their necks."

"Of course. There is a more elegant way, one that was engineered by Cramer in the very beginning, for this very situation."

"Cramer knew this would happen?"

"Everyone knew this would happen, eventually, if things Outside didn't improve, as we hoped they would. But it's certain death on the other side of that trapdoor—most likely a violent one. At least down here in the Shelter we can do it our own way. Keep our peace, and our dignity."

"So what was it? The elegant way to ... for us all to cross?"

"We'll use the gas," says William. "The same gas we use for cooking and heating our water. It has a timer that we can set. We'll have our last Crossing ceremony, we'll pray, and then we'll turn it on."

Caron sobs, and William pulls her into his arms and kisses the top of her head.

"I urge you to remain calm," says Adira. "And, if it's not too much to ask: *cheerful*. Keep in mind how blessed we have been to have this Shelter. Spend time with your loved ones tonight; talk about all the happy memories you share. Tomorrow a new journey begins."

. . .

The Dwellers begin dispersing. Some are weeping, some shrunken into themselves, afraid.

"Tomorrow a new journey begins?" whispers Anna. "Do you think she honestly means that?"

"No," says Simon. "But what else can she say? She's the Matriarch, it's the Ending, and she has to be gracious."

"Do *you* believe there is freedom in death?"

"I don't know. I think I've always thought so, with people crossing, but now … with baby Bella…"

"I won't do it, Simon," says Anna. Her face is flushed with defiance.

"What do you mean, you won't do it? Everyone has to do it. It's the Ending."

"I won't do it, I don't want you to do it, and I am certainly not doing it to Bella."

"Anna," says Simon, taking her hand. "You speak as if we have a choice."

"There is always a choice."

"The only other option is to starve—slowly—to death. We've been hungry for so long … let's not torture ourselves."

"There's another option," says Anna. "And it's hanging around our necks."

"What? Do you mean our keys? Do you mean … unlocking the door and going Outside?"

"Yes!"

"Anna. You are upset. You are not yourself."

"We have these keys for a reason. We've been wearing them since we were children!"

"They're symbolic, for god's sake."

"Yes, to remind us that we are not prisoners here. That we may leave at any time!"

"That locked door has kept the Marauders out, and us alive. I don't even know how you can consider going out there."

"I'm not considering it."

"But ... you just said—"

"I'm not considering it. I've already made up my mind."

"Anna, please," says Simon, taking her arms in both hands. "Listen to reason!"

"I will not die down here. I will not lie down quietly and have Bella die in my arms. I will not die not knowing what it feels like to be Outside."


Adira's heeled footsteps approach. "Anna, what are you saying?"

"Thank god, Adira. Anna listens to you. Please talk some sense into her."

"Think of it as a Crossing," says Anna. "My punishment, or ... my sacrifice for the Shelter. Instead of taking a noose around my neck, I will go Outside."

Anna sweeps her fringe out of her fevered face and keeps talking. "Worst case scenario, I will die just a few hours earlier than if I stayed down here. Best case scenario, I will find food and bring it down. Perhaps Cramer is dead, but perhaps his secret vegetable garden is still alive."

"It's too dangerous," says Simon.

"I've made up my mind."

"Well, then, I'm coming with you," he says. "There is no way you're going alone."

Bella's eyes flit open, then close again.

Adira's cheeks are now also pink. "Leave Bella with me. Caron will help me look after her until ... until you come back."

"Are you saying we can go?" says Anna.

Adira speaks softly. "You have never needed my permission."


Anna turns to Simon. "Let us go, now, before we lose our nerve."

Simon's face blanches, he puts his hand on Bella's blanket. "How does one even begin to say goodbye?"

"It's impossible," says Anna.

Simon wraps his arms around them and they stand like that for a minute.

"Adira, thank you," says Anna. "For everything. Bella ... goodbye my sweet girl. I'll come back for you."

She kisses Bella on her forehead and hands her to Adira.

"Goodbye," says Simon. "Goodbye, my Bella."

"May peace be with you," says Adira.

Simon and Anna reply together: "And with you."


They hurry to the trapdoor, their nerves stoking their starved hearts and muscles. They climb the narrow, musty stairs. Anna's foot slips, and she almost tumbles, but Simon holds her up. She takes her looped twine from around her neck and holds the key. The key she has spent nights warming and polishing and using as a portal to her dreams.


"This is a moment I have dreamt of so often," Anna whispers.

"I know," says Simon. His voice is gruff with fear.

"Here is my key."

She holds the key in her hand, reminds herself to breathe.

"Well," says Simon. "What are you waiting for?"

"I don't know," Anna says, a nervous twitch at her lips. "Certain death?"

"Probably," says Simon.

"I love you," says Anna.

"I love you too."


Anna looks up and inserts the key into the trapdoor lock, but it won't turn. The lock is stiff; grimy and rusted. She forces it, but worries her key may break and block the mechanism forever. Simon takes it from her and tries, but he can't turn it either.

Anna takes over again, pushing against the door as she wiggles and turns the key at the same time, and at last it crunches open.

She feels her adrenaline pumping through her body; rushing in her ears. They struggle to push the trapdoor open because it's covered with a huge carpet, but once there is enough space, Anna crawls out, rolls the carpet back, and the door opens freely. Simon climbs out from the Shelter and they lock the door again.

They stand in the near-dark and talk in hushed, excited whispers.

Anna sniffs the air. "You smell that? Fresh air!"

"Yes," says Simon.

"Fresh air! No matter what happens now, I have experienced fresh air. I am free!"

"At least the house is still standing. That's something. I wondered if we might come up to a razed building. Bombed, or burnt. Wait, look, down the corridor ... there's a light on."

"Cramer?"

"Can't be."

"Who else would be in Cramer's house?"

"I don't want to know the answer to that, but they could be dangerous. Let's get out of here. See if we can find the garden."

They move away from the light, towards the back door.

"It's so dark," says Anna. "I can hardly see anything."

She accidentally knocks an ornament off a side table and it crashes to the floor. She breaks into a cold sweat; her fingers turn numb. There is the sound of a chair scraping the floor in the room of light; footsteps.

"Hello?" comes an anxious voice. Male, with an accent Anna has never heard before. "Hello?"

"Hide!" says Simon. "Hide!"

"Hello?" calls the strange voice. "Is there someone there?"

A click of a switch and the passage is flooded with a sheer golden light that takes Anna's breath away. She freezes.

A tall man stops at the doorframe. "Jesus Christ!" he exclaims.

Anna is terrified. She puts her hands up and backs away from the man. "Please don't kill us," she begs.

She's too scared to look at his face. Thinks somehow if she doesn't look at him properly then he won't exist. Won't attack them.

"Please don't kill us."

The man is incredulous. "*Kill* you?"

"Who are you?" says Simon, stepping out from the shadows. "What are you doing in Cramer's house?"

"Who am *I*?" asks the man. "Who the devil are you?"

Anna braves a glance at him, and recognises the nose, the chin. "You're ... Cramer's son. I can see it in your face."

He frowns at them. "Yes, I'm Oliver Cramer. But who are—?"

"He told us you lived overseas, where it was safe," says Anna. "Where there was no Great War."

"I live in London. I'm here to tie up the estate ... and sort out the giant mess he left behind." He gestures at the old house. Now that the light is on, Anna sees the damp, peeling wallpaper and the lifting floorboards. The walls are smudged, and dust covers every surface. Shelter blankets cover the furniture.

Anna's mouth is open. "You were safe in another country and you came back to South Africa?

Oliver pushes his spectacles up the bridge of his nose and peers at her. "Why wouldn't I?"

"Civil war since the election. Starvation, disease," says Simon.

"The whole country has been ravaged, almost everyone killed," says Anna. "The Marauders!"

"Wait, what?" says Oliver. "Who are the Marauders?"

They stand and stare at one another.


"Look, where did you two come from? You're so pale ... you're practically ... glowing. And you—girl—you're wearing my old varsity shirt. Where did you get that from?"

"We're—"

"Oh. I get it. You're squatters. You've helped yourself. The house has been empty for a few weeks. It's bound to attract people like you."

"People like us?"

Anna takes a breath. "Cramer saved us from The Great War. He's been looking after us since it started."

Oliver is still. "My father ... saved you from what?"

"From The Great War. They were killing people like us. White people."

"Genocide," says Simon.

"He hid us in his basement. Kept us safe. Brought us food. We had to keep quiet or—"

Oliver shakes his head, and his fringe flops in his face. He holds his hand up in front of him. "I'm sorry, I still don't understand. What war?"

"The civil war that started in '94," says Simon. "Just before the new party came into power. Our street was bombed. That was the beginning of The Great War that destroyed the country."

"Cramer took us in," says Anna. "Protected us."

"Oh my God," says Oliver. "I think I need to sit down."

"He's a hero," says Simon.

"No," says Oliver. "No, he was not a hero. How did you escape?"

"Escape?" says Anna. "There was nothing to escape. We had the keys to the trapdoor the whole time. We didn't lock ourselves in, we locked The Great War out."

Oliver looks like someone has just slapped him.

"Do you have any food?" asks Simon.

"Food? Of course. You're both skeletal. Let's go to the kitchen. We'll have some tea."

Anna wonders out loud. "Tea?"

. . .

They pad down the passage, towards the room of light, which is the kitchen. Oliver switches on the vintage kettle and passes them the fruit bowl, then starts to raid the grocery cupboard. Simon starts loading the threadbare hessian bag they brought along. Anna stares at the kettle as it boils, wondering what these magical cords and switches are. She's never known anything brighter than candlelight.

"Here," says Oliver, handing them packets of food. "Eat this." He looks ashen despite the blasting yellow bulb above him.

"Thank you," says Anna. She desperately wants to eat one of the bananas. She can't remember the last time she ate a banana. Her mouth salivates at the sight of all the food on the counter. She catches sight of a loaf of soft bread. Bread!

"Don't worry about us," says Simon. "We're gathering food for the others."

Oliver looks faint. He grabs on to the kitchen counter. "Are you are saying ... there are others? Like you?"

"Six families altogether," she says. "Cramer saved six families."

"Oh my God! Where are they?"

"In the Shelter. Under the floor."

"He told me he had the basement sealed off," says Oliver. "He said there were rats. He covered the trapdoor with that Persian."

Anna feels her breasts tingle with milk. She needs to get back to Bella. "The others are waiting for us."

Oliver suddenly becomes animated. "We need to get them out

of there immediately. They can have all the food in the house. I'll buy more tomorrow."

"But is it safe?" says Anna. She wants to bring Bella up into the fresh air, but what if the Marauders come?

"Where will you get the food?"

Oliver coughs. "The grocery store!"

Anna and Simon look at him, unconvinced. Is he trying to trick them?

"There are still grocery stores?"

The kettle switches itself off, spooking Anna.

"Look ... sit down," says Oliver. "There's no easy way to say this. There was no war."

"Yes there was," says Anna. "People died. Our street was bombed! My parents died in the explosion."

Oliver looks at her with emotion in his eyes. "True, there was unrest in the build-up to the elections. Your street may have been bombed, some people died. But listen to me. There. Was. No. War." He looks her directly in the eyes, as if to force the knowledge to sink in. "South Africa is a peaceful democracy. You've been living in a basement for twenty years under ... false pretences."

"I don't believe you," says Anna.

"I'll take you outside right now and show you. It's a beautiful, peaceful evening."

Simon's face is marble. "We need to get the others out before they—"

"Of course," says Oliver. "Of course. Right away."

Anna starts trembling all over. She can't control it. "But Cramer said—"

"My father was a lonely man," Oliver says. "He was ill. If I had realised just how ill..."

He scrapes his fingers through his hair and shakes his head again. Anna has the idea that he's trying to dislodge the plague of hungry locusts she imagines are in his head.

She watches him reach for a black device on the counter and put it to his ear. Anna looks at the thing, puzzled.

"I'm calling for help," Oliver says, then as an afterthought: "This is a phone."

Anna blinks at him and thinks *we had the keys all along.*

She trembles and trembles, and Simon puts his arm around her shaking shoulders. "Let's go to the others. Let's get Bella."

## 4

# THE CHILDREN IN THE WALLS

THE RAIN COMES DOWN in a hot sheet, a wall of water that seems intent on keeping me out of the house. I fight through it, soaking my hair and thin T-shirt. My shoes are squelching silicone. Lightning scratches silver into the sky and shocks the old house with its blue-white light, electrifying the air as if it's saying *Danger! Stay Out.*

I push myself forward, regardless. I need to get in. The children are in there, alone.

A river of rainwater gurgles against my ankles. I dream of dry clothes and something to eat. Something dry and crispy and warm, to counter the sogginess: the water dripping from my hair and nose. Then I realise the children will be hungry, too, but I haven't brought any food along with me. My hunger mixes with dread now, a hunger-dread, and the combination makes my stomach twinge.

. . .

Eventually I push through the forcefield of weather so determined to keep me out and I stumble to the front door. The rain doesn't give up. Even under the shelter of the verandah it lashes at my legs and back as I jiggle the doorknob and bash the heel of my fist on the door.

"Hello?" I shout. "Hello?"

But the storm is thundering all around me, following me as if I am a lightning rod. As if it wants to smother me, or better: get right inside me, a dark grey cloud intent on swarming down my throat and into the brittle ribcage that is aching from containing my racehorse of a heart.

"Hello?"


The door is locked, and no one will hear me knocking, but I need to get in. I go back into the storm, into the mud and sodden weeds that used to be a garden, and find a rock. As I reach my hand out to pick it up, a bolt of lightning shears the air in front of me and I can't help shouting in shock. My body reverberates with adrenaline. I lift the rock; it feels warm in my hands, as if the current had struck it directly and bestowed some kind of dark magic. A totem; a magnet; a dirty charm. I carry it to the front of the house and smash a window pane with it. Then I take off my T-shirt, wrap it around my hand, and brush away the leftover daggers of glass. I force my body through the small frame, shucking my torso on the way through. The hornet-stings of glass-on-skin make me cry out, but the pain is worth the ticket in.


I land on old timber floors, dusty and dry, and wonder whether I should put my wet shirt back on. My pale, frayed skin is bleeding in long crimson ribbons, so I decide against it, and hang the wet cotton on the banister at the bottom of the stairs. The dripping sound it makes forces the hair on the back of my neck to turn to needles.

"Kids?" I call. "Abby? Chris?"

The storm sounds as loud inside the house as it was outside, and the blue flashes are just as bright. Calling for the kids won't help. I'll have to search. I don't want to go up the stairs so I'll start downstairs and hope they're tucked snugly in front of the TV, eating cookies and drinking warm, milky tea. Chris loves his tea, always has. He likes to crawl into my lap to nick my last tepid sip.

Walking along the passage, I avoid the broken floorboards and grimy walls. Without warning, a small black shadow darts into my hair. I shriek and try to comb it out. I feel its feet scramble on my scalp as it struggles to escape the moving cage of my fingers. Its wings flutter frantically, trying to get free, but its panicked movements only serve to tangle it more. I breathe in the animal's panic and a shot of adrenaline heats my veins.

I grab a pair of steel scissors from the writing desk and put the cold metal close to my scalp, cutting the hair that is trapping the baby bird, hoping not to injure it. I cut and cut, and tresses of my damp hair fall onto the floor around me, layered with small dirty feathers, and then eventually the bird is free. It shoots away, leaving me breathless, gripping the glinting blades of the scissors in the dim passage light, my limbs trembling, my scalp shorn.

. . .

My breath is shaky as I enter the TV lounge, but the children aren't there. Stuffed toys lie abandoned on the stained carpet. The hunger-dread is gnawing at my insides, growing bigger, stronger. The TV lies smashed on the floor. I try to flick on the lights, but somehow I know before touching the toggle that the bulbs won't come on. I jiggle it up and down, anyway, just to be sure. The house remains dark, apart from the flashes of blue current radiating through the windows.

"Kids?"

Deep down, I know they will not answer, just as I knew the lightbulbs would not wake up. I make my way into the kitchen, dreaming of finding them there, huddled at the kitchen table, spilling sweet cereal onto the old green embroidered tablecloth I inherited from my mother.

They're not in the kitchen. I put the scissors down and open the snack cupboard to see if there is anything I can eat to stave off this creeping, grasping dread I have clawing at my intestines. Something to feed the children. The hinge groans as I open the door, and I move closer to inspect the contents. Something jumps at me and suddenly there are animal thorns embedded in my face. Shocked and confused, I think the bird is back, but then I realise this thing is furry and has needles for claws. I scream and scrabble to get it off, and it squeals in my ear. Fright sucks the breath out of my lungs. Whiskers perforate my inner ear, and talons shred my eyelids and cheeks. The rat doesn't let go.

. . .

I scream louder and squeeze it, hoping to stun it into releasing my face, and as I apply pressure, the creature lands a vicious bite underneath my eye. My body wants to explode with horror and adrenaline. Its teeth are dirty razors; its whiskers scuttle in the most tender part of my ear. I have no choice but to squeeze harder. My hands are shaking, but I use all my strength to crush the attacker's body in my hand. Its squeal gets louder, and then off-key, and then there is a wet popping sound and the squealing stops, and it finally lets go.

I don't want to know what the popping sound was, don't want to look at the small still-warm body with its fat pink earthworm tail. I avert my eyes and toss it into the corner bin, and my hands fly up to my bleeding face. There is a deep gash where the rat sank its incisors, and I can't help imagining the bacteria inside the laceration, spreading like black poisoned ink beneath my skin. I need the first aid kit, but something tells me this house no longer has the emergency case I used to keep the cartoon plasters and disinfectant in. Instead I go rooting in the detergent cupboard.

Cockroaches scuttle away from my probing hands. Some of the bigger ones are too comfortable to flee and stay put, swirling and clicking their antennae together, daring me to grind their crunchy carapaces under my heel. I shudder as I rummage through the dusty bottles and cloths, afraid the beetles will scurry towards me and climb into my socks and up my legs, inside my jeans. I pull all the detergents out and they roll around on the hard floor like skittles. I find what I'm looking for

—a nondescript white bottle of bleach—and screw the cap off. I swallow hard, tilt my head back, close my eyes, and pour the sodium hydrochloride over my face. The bleach is like a hot knife on my broken skin and I hiss in pain as it bubbles over the fine cuts and needle-claw holes. When the stinging starts to settle, I use a soft orange cloth to wick away the excess, and dry my eyes, which are stinging from the chemicals. When the next flash of lightning lights up the kitchen I see my reflection in the fridge door. I don't recognise the face that stares back at me: bleeding; swollen; wild. Eyebrows bleached silver and a new stripe of white at my crown of jagged hair. The light disappears as quickly as it appeared and I am once again in the dark. I need to find the children.

They're not downstairs. I've been avoiding climbing the stairs but now I don't have a choice. The hunger-dread is now throttling me from the inside. Each step I take makes it worse, as if my anxiety is a creature trying to escape the confines of my stomach. A kraken intent on breaking out of my body and this house. Once it's free it will slither out the front door and find its way home. Will that be in the greasy black mud that surrounds this house, forever threatening to swallow it up, or will the creature be whipped up by the wind and find its home in the grey, swirling clouds? I blink away the futile wondering, the useless thoughts. I ignore the kraken's sucking tentacles on my insides and keep climbing up the stairs.

I reach the top floor and the storm roils outside. Abigail's room is empty. Her giant teddy bear is disembowelled and missing an eye. The bear's stuffing coats everything in the room, like snow. I have the urge to stop and look through her things: I want to smell her clothes and touch her soft security blanket to my face, but instead I force myself to continue, to turn my back on the bleak snowscape that is her room. Christopher's room is empty, too. I step inside and a cluster of spiders scatter, finding shelter in his cupboard, under his bed, in his wooden toy-box. The model plane that used to hang from the ceiling lies smashed on the floor.

The little hope I have streams out of my body. It's a tangible sensation, as if it is pulling my spine out from the back of my neck, and I collapse on the dirty floor and sob into the dust. I cough and splutter, and try to keep the vomit from spilling out of my mouth.

I want to shout *What happened?* but I know it will be of no use. I've been through this before, this turgid grey nightmare. A nightmare, yes, but it's not a dream. I know what it is, and I must keep going until I find my toddler, and my baby.

Then I hear them calling me. "Mama!" says Abigail. "Mom, mom," says Chris, and I jump up off the floor and run towards the sound. In my hurry I trip over a lifting floor-board and go sprawling down the passage, stitching my palms with fine splinters. Beads of blood appear. I deny the pain and keep going.

"Mom!" says Chris.

"I'm here!" I shout. "I'm here, I'm here! Where are you?"

I look in the linen cupboard and the children's bathroom, but they aren't there.

. . .

The storm screeches outside and there is a crack of lightning, and that's when I see them. Or I see their shapes, anyway. Like silhouettes, but more solid. The children are in the walls. I throw myself against the painted plaster and brick, trying to touch them, trying to wrestle them free from the house that has imprisoned them. My hands leave crimson smears on the walls; hieroglyphics of terror.

"Abby!" I shout, and my baby starts to wail. I smash my burning fists against the bricks, trying to break through.

"Chris!"

Chris doesn't try to break through the wall. He stands there with his arms at his sides. I need to find something to open the wall with. I don't have an axe. I don't even have a butter knife. I think about the scissors downstairs, but then I remember that they don't let us keep anything sharp here.


I so desperately need to see them, hug them, feel their sweet-scented skin on mine, but they are just out of reach. I cry and pound the walls; both the children are crying, now.

"No, Mama," says Abigail. "No!" She is sobbing and gurgling. I remember her thrashing against me in the water. The rain pours.

Chris is quiet. He's gone. He was first to go, because at three years old, he was the eldest. Abby disappears from the wall, now, too.

. . .

Both quiet now. Forever.

I'm on the floor and I crawl to my bedroom, where the dust is as thick as a carpet. I haul myself up and fight my way through the yellow police tape. It threatens to slither around my body and squeeze me, strangle my flesh, but I struggle against it and win. My prize is access to my bathroom, which brings everything back in striking detail. Suddenly the lights are on, and the house is no longer decrepit. There are colours in this world: a yellow rubber duck and a big bottle of pink bubble bath. Striped towels and pastel unicorn and rainbow pyjamas. You'd think it would be comforting to be back in this yellow light and humid soap-smelling air, but it's the opposite, because I know what happens next. I watch a younger version of myself appear with baby Abigail in her arms. She speaks to Abby in a comforting coo, but I can see her eyes are like cracked ice. Something inside her brain has fractured, and remains fractured, still.

She begins to undress the baby and I launch myself at her.

"Stop!" I scream. "Stop! Stop!" I shout as loudly as I can, but of course she can't hear me, and she can't feel my hands clawing at her, trying to keep her from hurting her daughter. My daughter. I scream and flail at the woman with my face—it looks like a mask, but I know it's real—and I think if I just focus intently enough I will be able to penetrate her reality and keep Abby safe. But no matter how much I grab and shout, nothing in the yellow-light world changes. She lowers the naked baby into the bath and I stop fighting and melt away. I can't witness it again.

Instead, I go to my bed and cuddle up to my son's cooling body. Chris has been dried and dressed in the soft rocket-ship dressing gown I know so well. I look at his eyelids, his beautiful long lashes, and sweep his tender body into an intense embrace and weep into his shoulder. I weep and weep, and then a shadow appears at the foot of the bed, holding a limp, dripping body, wrapped in a towel. I turn my back to the shadow, willing it to go away, but I know I can't deny her forever.

After all, this house is the prison I built for myself. It's in my head, but that doesn't make it any less difficult to inhabit. The concrete world now—the real world—is a white room with gentle nurses and three meals a day and three bars on the window. I don't deserve the food, so I don't eat it. Hunger-dread. I am unworthy of the comfort, the kindness, so I spend my days in this house with the children in the walls, instead.

## 5

# DEATH IS A WOMAN IN A BLUE DRESS

I wasn't supposed to let her in. I wasn't supposed to let anybody in. The world is a dangerous place full of people who mean you harm. I marvel at those who go outside into the chilled air, opening themselves up to being sneered at, attacked, stabbed with a sharp, cold knife. I decided long ago that it was much safer to stay indoors. I have my cats, and my things, and my television.

But even that decision didn't safeguard me, because people outside can come in, even if they're not invited. I didn't invite the woman in the blue dress, and yet here I lie on my threadbare bed, heart still, lungs cold slabs of jelly. The blood in my veins turned blue, then black. My mouth gapes open as if it's trying to swallow the sky.

After years of wishing to be alone, I now wish someone would find me. I worry about the cats, who I'm sure are hungry and thirsty, although I do not hear them cry. Left to their own devices they will catch a mouse, I know, or a lizard. They'll tongue the condensation from the grass, or the slow-dripping kitchen tap that I never got around to fixing, and now, never will. But I worry about them, still. I wish someone would find me.

I alienated everyone I used to be friends with. I stopped answering my phone and turned down invitations until I stopped being invited. Even my own flesh and blood, my children, don't visit anymore. I don't blame them. I wouldn't visit myself, either. That's a hard pill to swallow.

I wish I had had time to change my clothes before the woman in the blue dress arrived. I don't own a smart outfit, not anymore, but I do feel a twinge of shame when I look down at my body sheathed in this stained, lint-littered tracksuit. I wish I could cover my body up, at least. Throw a blanket over it, but I've learnt now that's not how things work.

I wish I had switched off the television. I used to like having it on all the time, but now it mocks me as I lie here. Teases me with its news headlines and adverts for irresistible weekend sales; dangling carrots I can no longer reach for. I like to buy things; collect things. I like to have things around me. They make me feel less lonely.

The things are another reason the kids don't like to visit. They used to pull disgusted faces when they were here, dangling one of my possessions in the air and crinkling their noses, as if it were a dead rat. *Jesus, Dad,* they'd say. *You need an intervention.* I told them all I needed was some peace and quiet, and children who respected their old man. Like I said, they don't come around anymore.

I worry about my things now that I'm dead. You wouldn't think I would, but I do. I worry that the reckless strangers I've been avoiding for so long will come in here and just smash everything down, bulldoze the place, and all my precious things will be lost. No one but me knows the value of my things.

On that day, the day it happened, I flinched when the doorbell rang. The idea of strangers at the door struck fear into my heart; the idea of friends visiting I found even more startling. Who was here? What did they want from me? I put my hands over my ears and rocked backwards and forwards. If I ignored them for long enough they would give up and go away. But the bell rang again and again, and I started to believe it was someone with bad news about one of the children, so I crept up to the door's peephole to see. And there she was: the woman in the blue dress.

There was something mesmerising about her, even through that small glass portal. She was utterly pale, and beautiful, and without thinking, my hand was on the door handle, pulling it down to let her in. Her eyes were dark crevasses and her raven hair smelled of apple orchards and decay, and yet I did not ask her to leave.

I did not welcome her, but I did not ask her to leave.

The woman didn't say anything to me, and I didn't speak. My tomcat, Blaise, hissed and snarled, but it didn't seem to worry her. He pounced at her ankles, tearing the delicate hem of her dress. The woman simply bent down and stroked him gently, and he fell into a deep sleep, which made me think of witches, good and bad, and fairytales curses.

She took my hand and led me to my room. A faraway part of my mind was racing with questions and urgent things to do, but mostly I was hypnotised; lulled into a deep calm. I knew instinctively what was happening, and what to do. I lay down on the bed.

The woman did not appear to be evil, like the death-grinning attackers that frighten my dreams. She wasn't here to assault me or steal my things. She was here to give me a gift, and I was ready. She stood at my bedside and I looked up at her, still stunned by her presence. She held my right hand in her left, smiled tenderly at me, and with her free hand swept my eyes closed. I felt my breathing slow, and my heart start to drift. It wasn't long before my blood stopped pulsing.

I expected to lose all consciousness then—forever—or be tempted to a new realm: a shimmering afterlife. But I can't seem to leave this room. I'm still tied to this body, tied to these things. So I just lie here and try to ignore the incessant blare of the television. I lie here and think of my cats and the woman in the blue dress. I'm not sure what happens next.

## 6

# FENRIR

NORWAY, 835 AD

"Bring us some more wine, boy," says Halstein, emptying his drinking horn as if it's a thimble of dandelion dew. Stig doesn't need to be asked twice. He scampers down the hall. Colborn approves.

"May as well finish our supplies before tomorrow's expedition," Halstein says. His face is full of firelight; his voice is as big as his barrel-chest. He fills his horn again with his clumsy bear hands, neither noticing nor caring how much of the expensive drink he spills. "To the feaste!"

"Aye!" shouts Fiske. "To the feaste! *Skål!*"

*Skål! Skål!* The cheers rise in the air like arrows.

Colborn joins in the merriment despite the feeling of dread in his bowels. He looks around him, as if for the first time, as if he is a stranger in this longroom which is usually as familiar to him as his own house. He gazes, with a new flicker of tenderness, at Stefnīr. His wife catches his eye and swings her foot, kicking his ankle with a grin. He watches Stig heave another great log onto the red coals. When did the boy shoot up like that? He was just yesterday a babe, mewling and suckling, growing like cotton-grass in summer. Now the imp is as tall as a crucible sword.

The Norse men, women and children are all painted warm by the flames in the hearth and in their heads. All manner of food is set before them: pickled duck eggs, cracked and marbled with beet, salted seal-meat, horse fillet from the roasting spit. Stig hurries back to the table balancing two bottles of wine as carefully as if his life depended on it. Halstein takes them from the barefooted boy and rewards him with a back-pat that nearly sends him flying. He stumbles on the woven wattle of the floor, but he is smiling.

"Come here," says Stefnīr. People usually listen to Stefnīr, even those not of her womb, even those older and stronger than she. Before Stig reaches his mother, Colborn lunges for him, drags him, protesting, onto his lap. He musses the straw on his head that passes for hair, his mother's hair. *My eyes though*, thinks Colborn, *and my nose. It's fairer on him than it is on me.*

Halstein leers at Stefnīr. "Give the boy some mead."

"He's too young," says Stefnīr. "He hasn't yet seen five winters."

"Too young?" booms Halstein. "I was fighting Saxons when I was his age."

"Aye, aye," she says, stretching her neck. "I'm sure you were."

The clanspeople laugh.

"I was!" he says. "They used to call me Stalwart Stein. My job was to spear the heads of the monks."

Stig looks up at the man, lips ajar.

"Father would give me a copper coin for every skull I spiked," Halstein says. "Before long I was chopping them down me-self.

How do you think I got to become a Jarl? My purse of Saint Peters started when I was half the size of Stig."

Colborn catches Stefnīr rolling her eyes; he runs his hand over her back.

"If only yer cock was as swollen as yer battle tales," says Ingvar. There is a sudden stiltedness in the festivities. Halstein frowns at his wife and at the rest of the table. Ingvar stares back at him, sparks in her eyes. The guests busy their gazes elsewhere, wicker-watching. They know better than to show their mirth. But then he tips his great black beard back and roars with laughter. The others take his cue and do the same. Stig doesn't understand the bawdy humour — not yet — but he chuckles with an open maw to join in the fun. Colborn hugs him closer. The boy squirms away and off his father's legs to grab at the honey-smoked hen's leg Stefnīr dangles in front of him.

"We'll sail before sunrise?" Colborn asks his leader. Over the years, as Halstein's girth has grown, so has he appreciated his morning slumber more. The next-to-last expedition saw Colborn having to lever the Norseman off his bench and onto the longboat, his lolling tongue still black with the previous night's wine.

"It's good to leave while the moon is still bright," Colborn says.

"Aye, aye, brother," says Halstein. "And it's a good thing, too, having you keep us on the narrow."

Colborn picks up a sharp henbone from his wooden bowl and uses it to pick errant flesh from his teeth. Under the table, Stefnīr palms the hard muscle of his thigh. This is how they speak, mostly. Through skin-grazing and gesture. It's the best way. The most honest.

*Let's get back, then,* her hands are saying. *We don't have much time. I want you to myself.*

They fuck once near the entrance of their longhall, Stefnīr pinned up against the daub, and again in bed on the furs. He watches her, astride him, the strength of her body, the softness of her breasts, as she climbs towards her zenith. She makes as much music as she likes. Stig has stayed over at Halstein's feaste. He wanted to hear the minstrels and gleemen play.

Once they are sated, Stefnīr rolls off Colborn and cleans herself. She uses her antler comb on her yellow mane. She comes back to bite his chest, to tickle his ribs and he swats her away. She laughs her lusty laugh, the sound that made him fall in love with her. In moments like this he wonders what he has done to deserve her. He turns to blow out the tallow candle when she stops him.

"You'll be careful tomorrow?"

"Aye," he says. "Always."

"You'll mind yourself?"

"Of course."

"Then I'll give you something to take with you." She bites him again, hard, leaving a leaf-shaped mark on his chest. "There," she says, rubbing the saliva away. "Now you can look at that and think of me."

"You witch," he says, "tormenting your man the night before he sails."

"Tormenting? Is that what we're calling it, now?"

Colborn laughs.

They move closer together so that Stefnīr's head rests in the crook of his arm, and they can look facewards. Colborn's hand lies on his wife's sure hip. She holds his other hand — sex-scented — near her lips.

"Don't go," she says.

"That's what you always say," says Colborn. "And I always come back, don't I, with silver and livestock and... fur blankets."

"We have enough of all that. The farm is in good stead. You'll see, come Harvest time, how much grain we have to store. We'll have more than enough. Besides, I'd rather have you here than all the silver in Essex."

"You're forgetting one thing," says Colborn. "I'm a warrior, not a farmer."

"You could be a farmer.'"

"You know it's not like that. I'm Halstein's second."

"More like you're the leader and it's only fat Halstein who hasn't realised it yet."

"*Och.*"

"It's true. He's not half the man you are. Everybody knows it."

"Aye, well, it's not a sport. He is welcome to his command."

"You won't stay? Even for Stig?"

"I can't stay and you shouldn't be asking me to," he says, taking his hand away.

"Don't be angry. I only ask because I want you. Not like Ingvar, who I'm sure would push Halstein straight out of the door and into the ocean if she could. You're my family; I won't lose my family again."

Stefnīr's mother died birthing her; she had lost her father in a raid.

"I'm not angry," Colborn says. "It's just..."

"Just?"

She steals his hand back. Kisses it.

"It's just that this time I feel it, too."

"What?"

"That I shouldn't get on that boat."

Stefnīr pushes herself up on her elbow, makes wide eyes at him.

"Then for Thor's sake, don't go!"

There is blood in her cheeks.

"You know as well as I do that our death days are already decided by the gods. Getting on a boat won't change that. It's just a feeling. A stupid feeling."

"Maybe you should listen to that stupid feeling."

He falls on his back, examines the rooftree.

"Like I did, when I married you?" he says.

"Aye," she says, "and look how that worked out for you."

She lies back down again, close. She traces the tattoo of the bite-mark, then strokes the silver wolf's head on its leather cord on his chest.

"My Fenrir," she says. "My moon-snatcher. My lone wolf."

The charm, a pretty wolf's head, had been a gift to her from her father. It was all she had of his. On their wedding day, after they had exchanged swords and rings, Stefnīr had strung the brooch and given it to Colborn. He had uttered the beginning of a refusal, but she had insisted and had tied it around his neck herself.

"It feels right," she had said. "Do you feel it?" and he had. He still does. He calls it his lucky charm.

Now Stefnīr moves to blow out the flame.

"No," he says, stopping her. "I want to look at you."

The candle burns all night.

At first light the longboat is keen and gleaming in its new clinker skin: the moulded gunwale is polished with beeswax, the woollen square-sail is dry and ready. The air around the North-men is still blue as they grip their oars; the white-breathed thralls push them into the tide. The men are excited and bang their burnished shields. They exchange happy insults as they row. Colborn leans against the bulwark and swallows the last of the elderberry tonic Stefnīr prepared for him hours earlier. It was green with fresh peppermint from their farm, to help settle his stomach, which never enjoyed the roiling of the sea.

"Drinking yer witch's potion again," says Halstein, uncharacteristically bright-eyed for this time of morning. Perhaps last night they had run out of ale.

"Aye,'" says Colborn, throwing the empty swine bladder into the stern-hold.

"Lower the flags!" he shouts, and the seafarers lower the handsome gold-woven Raven banners: the two black birds of blood fold down as if being put to sleep. *Huginn* and *Muninn* — thought and memory — are laid to rest so that the men can approach the Saxons without alerting the sentinel. Although he has seen this many times before, the image stays with Colborn. Something feels different: a premonition that one way or another, this will be his last expedition.

"Now, hear ye, men," shouts Halstein, half an hour away from their landing spot. "It's time to get clear of purpose."

"Aye, aye," say the Vikings. They blow their noses into the sea and rotate their shoulder cuffs. Their feet won't stay still.

"Before ye grab yer breastplates and blades," says Halstein, "I want ye to hear me."

The men keep moving their limbs, keeping supple, but their attention is now on their leader.

"We'll be landing in the Isle of Sheppey where ye know we invaded last Spring."

"Aye," says Fiske. "It was a good haul, Sheppey."

"Aye," say the Norse raiders. "Aye."

"Now we were very kind to them then and didn't spill much blood, but they will be better prepared this time. They'll have weapons and a plan."

The pirates nod and flex their bodies.

"This time you will show no mercy. No hesitation. I won't lose one man, ye hear? Not a one."

"Aye," the men say.

"Ye hear me? Is it clear to ye? No mercy!"

"Aye!" shout the seafarers. "No mercy!"

"I want ye to kill every man you see. Take what they have. And do what ye will with the wenches."

The men whistle, show their tongues and pant like horny dogs. Fiske humps the dragon-fashioned stern and there is high laughter.

"I want ye men to frighten every Saxon ye see. Knock the heads off the men. Terrify the women and children."

"Hold on," says Colborn, tasting the salt in the air. "Hold on. Why will we now hurt the women? The children?"

"Because, Colborn, the more we scare them in this battle, the less resistance we will find in the next." Halstein lifts his bear claw in Colborn's direction. The men quiet down.

"You have a problem with my tactics? Speak now."

"I don't agree with wounding the women unless they pose a danger."

"Ah, lads," Halstein says, fingering his beard. "Get out yer big fat tears. Take yer wails out of yer pockets. It looks like our Colborn here has grown a cunt."


The warship glides onto the tide-flattened beach with a whisper of polished wood greeting sand. The anchor, a rock lashed to a branch and fixed there, is lowered into the shallow brine. The spear-armed men hop off the stern with unexpected grace and fly up the dune like marauding monkeys. Steel glints. Even the seagulls are silent.

Colborn pats his helmet down onto his head and runs along the beach, just ahead of the other marauders. He begins to feel the adrenaline, the vibrating energy, in his limbs. The part of him that is happy husband and loving father separates from his body and flies above him like a calfskin kite. That part cannot do the job of the warrior. That part cannot endure the shock of war. He feels the hot blood beginning to beat in his ears. He sniffs. He gnashes his teeth. He is animal. He is Fenrir.

The first of their victims are fishermen taking stock of their day's haul. Five men smelling of cod and seagrass fall to the earth at the same time, hands wrapping around the strange new arrow-shafts planted in their chests as the tangs shock their hearts. More fishermen and more well-placed arrows until they reach the settlement of huts and halls with turf for roofs.

A woman stirring the steaming contents of an iron cauldron atop a kindling fire looks up and sees the army. She drops the spoon and screams, until an arrow finds its way into her chest. Now their shroud of silence falls to the ground. The raiders shout and bite their shields. Spears wing through the air. Cries, both shrill and deep, pierce the land along with swords and spikes and long-handled axes. Creamy throats are slit open, bodies fall into mud.

Colborn cuts down his twelfth Christian: a padded man who was swinging some kind of stick at him. Colborn feels no fatigue in his sword-arm or in his fighting spirit. Here is another Saxon who doesn't stand a chance. Colborn impales the man without hesitation or pity. All around him there is shouting and moaning and the clashing of steel on steel and steel on bone. Red ribbons of blood spurt skywards like a gory Maypole dance. Meaty maroon mixes with mud. Colborn kills another man, and another. He has a dark power rushing through him. He is a giant. He is a conquerer. He is in the prime of his life. He stabs a curly-haired leather-tanner, and a blacksmith in a scorched tunic. The darkness is like a swarm of black bees in his veins, in his head, pushing him to keep killing, keep plundering. It's like a pair of giant bat wings driving him forward. He slashes and steals and stabs until he is ankle-deep in greasy clay and treasure and still-warm bodies.

And then there is a woman's face in his, her cheek smeared with soil and crimson. She won't let him enter her hut. He pushes her aside but she is stubborn and flings herself back into his path. He smacks her head, hard, and she cries out and falls at his feet. Even so assaulted, she hangs onto his legs to hinder him. Colborn is overcome with fury. The black bees pour into his head, blotting out all reason and rationality. He bends at the knees and roars.

"Terrify the women!" he hears Halstein yell. It's a requisite; a battle tactic. It will cause future fights to be less cruel. It will mean less blood leaking into the ground. It's his duty to show this wench her place. The fury makes him kick the woman up, off his shins and he grabs her arms and jettisons her against a giant standing rock.

"No!" she screams into his face. Her ear is bleeding from his blow.

Colborn squeezes her against the stone: a warning to stay back now while he raids her hut. He loosens his grip and turns towards her home.

"No!" she screams again, falling after him and Colborn loses his temper.

"Terrify them!" a phantom Halstein roars in his ear. The bees in his head and veins buzz wildly and take over his body. He slams her against the rock again and tears off her shift, revealing full, white, milky breasts. Before he knows it, his cock is in his hand and he is forcing it under her dress and into her flesh. She cries out in horror and in pain. She scrabbles at his neck, tries to dig her nails into his throat. He grips her hands and pins them back against the stone while he finishes attacking her. There is no pleasure in his orgasm. It feels obligatory, like a spurt of warm blood once an artery has been ruptured. Colborn pulls away and tucks himself back into his trousers. His anger is gone; he feels disorientated. Did this just happen? The woman's mask of horror assures him that it did. He will plunder this home now. He will get what he has fought for.

She tackles him; grabs hold of his ankle. There is no anger left in him. He hauls her up and head-butts her with his iron helmet. She melts away into the mud.

*"Brenna!"* comes the call. "Burn! Burn! Burn!"

It's time to go and to leave the village afire. The homes all around him become lamps. Suddenly, whatever wealth this particular hut hides, no longer appeals to him. He wants nothing of it; no reminder of today's battle. He feels the need to flee, to get back to the longboat and the seawater and just row, row, row, until they are at home and at peace and he can hold his wife and son again.

His neck is bleeding: his fingers come away incarnadine. The skin on his throat is a knot-work pattern of fingernail cuts. How will he explain it to Stefnīr?

102

Fiske marches past, handing him a flaming brick of hay. Colborn holds the firelighter to the thatch of the hut, lights it in three places. Let it all burn, he thinks. Reduce it to ashes. I never want to think of this day again.

The roof begins to crackle and steam. There is a searing surge of furious flame. The fire gains momentum quickly like a body rolling down a hill. Pieces of fire drop down into the interior and eat up what is inside. Colborn feels the wall of heat against his chainmail, his helmet. He steps back to ease the burn and, as he does so, he hears something; a strange sound. He shakes his head and hears it again. Is it a lamb protesting at being dragged onto the boat? No, it's coming from this bonfire in front of him. A choking sound. Screaming. Was there an animal inside? He steps forward again to look through the tiny opening in the wall. His armour takes on the heat of the fire and bites into his skin, blistering his torso and forehead. That's when he sees the wooden crib on fire. Sees the crying baby in it.

His instinct is to barrel into the furnace, scoop the burning baby up, but he knows it's too late.

Too late for the baby, who dies right then before him as the house turns into a ball of fire.

Too late for the baby's mother whom he has all but destroyed.

Too late for himself, because all his loving and valorous moments fall away like old scales as this horror becomes his defining moment and he cannot live with that. Cannot bear a future of looking backwards, of seeing this window-framed picture of cruel burning cot, cradle set on fire by his very hands. He won't be able to bear touching Stefnīr or Stig with these self-same hands. And what is a life if he can't do that?

He grabs at his injured throat for the silver wolf's head. He needs to touch it to remind himself of who he is. But it is gone. Torn off in the assault. He has lost it because he doesn't deserve it any more. He falls to his knees and pushes his hands into the mire. He trails his fingers through the blood and sand hoping to rake up the leather thong. Fire falls all around him, as if from the sky, from the gods. The smoke makes his eyes water and tears stream down his battle-smeared face. As he sinks further down his hot armour is cooled by the mud. His soul keens. Fenrir is lost.

That is how Halstein finds Colborn, weeping in the dirt.

"Well," Halstein says, leaning against the great standing stone and taking in the unconscious woman and the defeated warrior, admiring the bruising on both. "Isn't this a pretty picture?"

Colborn has offered Halstein a hand up on so many occasions when Halstein has found himself sprawled on the wattle, post-feaste, wine-drunk. Halstein does not return the favour.

"Everyone is on the warship," he says, "spoils included. All there but one."

"Go," says Colborn. "Go without me."

Halstein spits on the ground. "No," he says, "I won't. It won't end like this."

"Just go," says Colborn, on his knees.

"I didn't come to find you to take you back on the boat."

Colborn looks up at him. Halstein is iolite in the dusk. White moonshine smoke trails up behind him. His sword is drawn. He looks like nothing less than a god: Odin.

He has something in his fist; something he has taken off the rock: a silver charm. Fenrir.

"Now Fenrir bit off the right hand of his god," says Halstein. "Then Víðarr laid waste to the wolf. That's the way the story ends."

"Aye," says Colborn, "that's the way it ends."

"You would have been better off," says Halstein, "if you hadn't challenged me in front of the men. If you hadn't bitten off my right hand."

"Aye. And, more to the point, I would have been better off if I hadn't married Stefnīr."

"Aye. That was your first and most fatal mistake."

"My second mistake was trusting a friend," says Colborn.

Halstein laughs.

"I don't see any friends here."


Colborn braces himself. He thinks of his farm under a clear sky and his impish, barefooted Stig. He sees Stefnīr's sweet, warm skin as if she is right in front of him. He hears her laugh and feels her biting his chest as Halstein runs his crucible sword through his ribs. The ravens shriek.

There is no pain, just the emptying out of the black bees and an exhalation as the evil leaves him. Colborn has already departed the realm when his body topples over next to the woman's. It will be her sole comfort when she wakes.

# 7

## LUCKY STRIKE

STUART IS IN AN EXCELLENT MOOD, humming and whistling along to the 80s music rattling my car's speakers as we twist and turn up the mountain road lined with dark-needled pine trees. He catches me looking at him and grins, taking his hand off the gear stick to caress my thigh. Despite it being chilly, I've worn the blue summer dress that clings to my body in all the right places. That's how Stu describes it, anyway. The skin on my leg erupts in goosebumps. I reluctantly close the window—the scent of the pines is wonderful—and pull my cardigan tightly around me.

"Don't worry," says Stuart.

I try to relax my face; smooth out the frown I see in the car's side mirror. I don't want to appear anxious.

"About what?" I ask.

"About being cold. As soon as we get there I'm going to warm you right up."

I plaster on a smile. I've never been very good at acting but Stu doesn't seem to notice.

"I am so looking forward to this weekend," he says. "I've been wanting to take you away for months. Somewhere special."

Stuart always tells me about the trips he wants to take me on, but they never materialise. He says his job is too demanding. I can't blame him, really. I'm not easy to pin down, either. I'm forever flitting from job to job, changing the cut and colour of my hair, and moving house. I'm a gypsy, a nomad, a weed that throws down only shallow roots. My passport is always in my pocket, but I never let Stuart see it.

Stu and I usually only get to see each other in snatches of time, but this weekend will be different. Every now and then, if you want something to happen, you have to take things into your own hands.

"Well," I say, "this time it's my treat."

The corner of his eyes crinkle as he smiles warmly at me. "Sometimes you just strike it lucky, you know?"

"You always say that."

"I mean it," he says, squeezing my knee. "It's true. You're my lucky strike."

There are some rocky slips of road to navigate, and wet sand flecks the car.

"This place really *is* in the middle of nowhere," says Stu, and I nod. It's exactly what I wanted. After another twenty minutes of negotiating the yellow dust and ricocheting gravel, we arrive at our accommodation: a small stone house that looks as if it's been swallowed by the plants and wildlife around it. As if it's in the mouth of a giant Venus Flytrap.

"Where's the owner?" he asks. "How do we get in?"

I walk up to the doormat and lift it. Wood lice scurry as I pick up the simple silver key. It glints in the citrus light of the sinking sun.

Inside, the house is decked out with large furniture, and lots of blankets and cushions. There is a fireplace next to the bed, which is a gigantic cast-iron thing—exactly as it showed on the website—and a lovely thick rug on the floor.

Stuart groans as he carries my luggage in. "What's in this thing?" and "How long exactly are you planning on staying?"

He likes to pack light, but I had certain things I needed to bring. Plus, there are some things I always keep in my car: a handheld vacuum, a torch, a tow-rope, a first aid kit.

"You can leave the big suitcase in the car," I call. "I just need the small one for tonight."

I unpack the cooler bag: the red wine, the bottle of vodka. When Stu sees the vodka he looks impressed. "I didn't realise it was going to be *that kind* of weekend."


Stu unpacks his clothes and toiletries and then opens a bottle of wine. He lights the fire while I close the curtains and then we sit in front of the flames and sip our merlot. He sighs and pushes his sleeves up his arms—smug—like the cat who caught the canary.

"This is really wonderful, Mandy," he says.

"It's perfect," I say. "No interruptions."

Stuart puts down his glass and growls at me. A bear in heat. "Come here," he says, flames in his eyes.

I shake my head. "No."

"No?"

"You're going to have to wait."

"Wait?" Stu says. "For what? Till when?"

"Till I say."

"Oh." Amusement flickers on his face. "I see. It's going to be like that."

"Yes," I say, trying to keep a straight face. "It's going to be like that."

I make Stuart wait for another hour, until we've finished the first bottle of wine and feel warm and tipsy. I tease him with allusions of what I will be doing to him later, and soon he can't keep his hands off me.

"Wait," I say, peeling his fingers off me.

"I can't wait any longer."

I push him away and go to the second bedroom to change. When I open the door, Stuart is lying on the bed in his silk boxers. His desire is clear.

"Holy shit," he says, looking me up and down.

I'm wearing a teal satin bodice with a padded push-up top. It cinches my waist and makes my breasts bloom. My arms are lined with soft black satin: elegant elbow-length gloves that I keep for special occasions. I feel as powerful and sexy as hell. Over the lingerie is my short silk robe. The right hand side pocket bulges slightly, but if Stuart notices, he doesn't say anything.

I sashay towards him, slowly, slowly, drawing it out and enjoying the feeling of his eyes on my skin. His mouth goes slack, his eyes burn. I arrive at the bedside and he reaches out to touch me, but I swat his hand away and climb up onto the bed and on top of him, spreading my legs to kneel on either side of his torso, sitting just above his hips, and run my hands along his chest.

He tries to touch my breasts but I grab his hands and thrust them above his head, against the iron bars of the bed, and kiss him deeply, luxuriously, so that he feels it right down to his core. He groans into my mouth, and it makes my body thrum.

"Now," he says. "I need you now."

I keep his wrists against the iron bars with my left hand as I rhythmically move my body against his. The friction makes him harder. With my right hand I reach into my pocket and soon there is a cold click above his head. Confused, he looks at his wrists just as I click the second handcuff closed. His face is soft with desire, but uncertainty scuds over it, like clouds racing over the sun.

"Oh, shit," he says.

*Oh shit is right.*

"I wasn't expecting that."

I look deep into his eyes. They are still reflecting the flames in the hearth.

"Are we going to ... play a game?" he asks.

"I'm tired of playing games," I say, and I climb off him.

"What?"

"Do you recognise them?" I ask. "The cuffs?"

"What?" he says again, and looks at them. They have a soft leopard-print fur covering to prevent chafing. They are not new.

Stuart whips his head from his trussed wrists to look at me.

"What the fuck?" His confusion is eroded by anger, and his cheeks burn. "What the fuck, Mandy?"

He thinks Mandy is my real name. I've always known that he's not the brightest sparkler in the pack.


"So you do recognise them," I say.

He shakes his head. The muscles in his jaw tense, sculpting his face with fury.

"I don't know what you—"

"Tell me whose handcuffs they are, Stuart. I want to hear you say her name."

"It's impossible," he says. "How did you—"

"I want to hear you say your mistress's name."

He glares at me with glass eyes.

I wait, not so patiently. I cross my arms and tap my stilettos.

A whisper escapes his shrunken mouth. "Annabel."

"Yes," I say. "Annabel."

"Did you ... hurt her?"

"Not as much as you did."

"Fuck. Mandy." He rattles his wrists against the iron bedstead. "This isn't funny. Let me go."

*I want to say:* I'm not laughing, *but I don't. I won't waste words on him. Not anymore.*

"Where are the keys?" he demands.

I blink at him. "Do you really want to know the answer to that?"

I had so many ideas as to what to do with the handcuff keys. Throw them into the rushing river I knew we'd visit on the drive here, or out of the window of my car, into the black-needled carpet under the fragrant pines.

He coughs in shock. "You can't just ... leave me like this."

"Can't I?"

For the first time, the gravity of the situation dawns on Stuart, and his eyes stretch wide.

"You wouldn't," he says.


I shrug and pick up the bottle of vodka, spin open the top. I soak a soft white muslin cloth in the spirit and begin wiping the furniture down. I vacuum the couch and the floor as Stuart stares open-mouthed at me: a gasping fish. When I'm sure I've wiped all my fingerprints and swept up any trace of my being there, I sprinkle some of Annabel's DNA over the floor, and in the bathroom sink. I leave the fingerprints on the handcuffs. Perhaps next time she'll take more care with where she stores her box of sex toys.

When I visited Annabel's smart apartment it reeked of her arrogance. Sex-stained panties in the laundry hamper, a laptop that required no password, credit card details saved in her browser. A gift tag stuck to the fridge door, in Stuart's handwriting, addressed to *My Lucky Strike*. I spent less than twenty minutes there, gathering what I needed and booking this cabin. Her hairbrush was tangled with her distinctive red hair, and her foot scrubber had plenty of dead skin cells I could scrape off.

I change into jeans and a hoodie, and pack my things back into the car, next to my big suitcase. I pat my pocket with my passport in it, then go inside to say goodbye.

"You can't leave me like this," he says. "Please. Mandy."

I want to leave before he starts to beg. I don't want to remember him like that.

"Where are the keys?" he says, pulling at the handcuffs.

"The keys?" I say. "They're at Annabel's apartment. In a neat white envelope on her kitchen counter, along with the booking confirmation print-out of this place. I'm sure she'll be on her way shortly."

I step outside the front door, and take a deep breath of the forest air.

"Mandy!" Stuart shouts. "Mandy! Annabel's away for a week! She won't get the envelope in time!"

"Ah, well," I say under my breath as I climb into the car, adjusting the rearview mirror. "Sometimes you just strike it lucky."

～

## 8

# THE HOSTAGE SITUATION

*FACEBOOK POST, Friday, 3 November 2017*

Whenever something goes wrong in my life, in order to gain perspective, I think: at least my children are healthy. That changed this weekend.

Baby Alex had a runny nose on Wednesday, was chesty on Thursday (but still well enough to run around with her brothers and eat dinner). On Friday morning at around 5:00, after a tough night of her not settling, her breathing became laboured, so we took her to the nearest hospital.

I wasn't panicking. I thought a quick steroid nebuliser would sort her out and that we'd be home in an hour. The first assessment wasn't too bad. The doc gave her a saline neb and recommended we go to a hospital with a paediatric unit. On our way downstairs to meet Mike she saw that the Swift Care / ER had an opening and asked the doc on duty to have a look at her before we left.

While the ER doc was assessing Alex, something changed. She got scared and started screaming and things started falling apart. She was in severe respiratory distress. The doc gave her a shot of adrenaline in the thigh and a steroid nebuliser. She battled to find a vein for the IV and that made Alex scream louder. I was just holding her, trying to comfort her, and she kept shouting for me. Eventually the doc got the needle in the other hand and they strapped it up, and she said she thought Alex was stable enough to be moved.

Sometime during the chaos, the paramedics arrived. Just as a precaution they'd be ready to intubate on the road if necessary. They put us on the stretcher and shuttled us into the ambulance, then delivered us safely to Sandton Clinic where there was a team waiting. The head paramedic (I don't remember anyone's names; I was operating in survival mode and just had the white static of anxiety in my head) was especially brilliant. So much warmth and empathy and he talked me through the whole thing, keeping me in the moment so that I wouldn't be overwhelmed by what was happening.

The nurses set Alex up with oxygen, X-rays, bloods, swabs, nebs ... and are kind to her even though she screams at whoever comes near her (traumatised by the needle in ER, I think). Docs think it's asthma but are running tests and we should know more, soon.

. . .

This morning she seemed much better so the nurse disconnected her IV and oxygen and let her walk to the playroom. She strolled down the corridor with a bounce in her step, and greeted everyone with a "HULLO!" and soon became the most popular patient in the ward.

Things were looking up but then she had two nosebleeds, had to go back onto oxygen, and then she had another attack. More adrenaline, more nebs, more screaming and railing against the tubes that are keeping her confined to bed. It's going to be another long night, but right now she's safe and asleep and I'm drinking tea and writing this, because anyone who's had a child in hospital knows how dread-lonely it is, and how comforting it is to share these experiences.

Moments I'll never forget:

Seeing the paramedics come into the small assessment room and thinking "They've got the wrong room."

Blood on Alex's dummy.

The reassuring weight of her body on my chest as she slept this afternoon, like she has so many times before. Stroking her damp curls while breathing in her perspiration and her nebuliser breath, and thinking how lucky I am, and how unlucky, and again, how lucky.

*Facebook post, Sunday, 5 November 2017*

Day 3 of the hostage situation and Baby Alex is ready to chew through her tubing to escape.

~

*Facebook post, Sunday, 5 November 2017*

Baby Alex's new favourite word: "Uh-oh."

~

*Facebook post, Sunday, 5 November 2017*

Baby Alex has turned the corner!

Literally and figuratively. She's on a trial break from the oxygen and is running around the ward, singing nonsense songs and shouting 'HULLO!' at everyone again, despite it being an hour past her bedtime. After days of not eating she had her whole dinner and half of mine, and she can chuckle without coughing.

~

*Facebook post, Monday, 6 November 2017*

Day 5 of the hostage situation and the prisoner has escaped her bed shackles and discovered The Snack Bag.

*Facebook post, Tuesday, 7 November 2017*

Day 6 of the hostage situation and the prisoner is showing marked signs of Stockholm Syndrome, smiling and high-fiving her captors despite their torture tactics and refusal to let her go.

～

*Facebook post Wednesday, 8 November 2017*

Day 7 of the hostage situation: The prisoner has taken to wearing the coolerbag on her head, perhaps in an attempt to fool her captors into letting her toddle, undetected, out the door.

～

*Facebook post, Friday, 9 November 2017*

PRISON BREAK.

～

## 9

## EVERY BREATH YOU TAKE

THE GUARD PUSHES the convict forward. This prison block is noisy; the kind of noise that coats your brain and stuffs up your nose. There's no escaping it. Men talking testosterone; tin cups clanging on iron bars; a payphone receiver being smashed against the chafed venom-green box. Someone laughs, someone shuffles a deck of cards, someone groans in pain—or pleasure— sometimes it's difficult to tell which.

The guard and the convict walk down the long passage, past the second storey cells, past the hands with dirty bruised fingernails waving from the locked stalls. The guard is bristling with weapons and duty gear. Flashlight; mag pouch; swivel holder with radio; pepper spray; handcuffs hooked into its single-snap strap. His gun, of course, and a badge wallet that carries flattering photos of his two snotty children at home. He carries his baton in his hand, the stop nestled into his damp armpit. The prison guard doesn't walk around here without at least one weapon ready to use, whether the cons are locked in or not. He's seen the damage they can do firsthand and won't take the chance. As he jokes with his wife: he's already ugly enough without getting his face rearranged. *Maybe it will be an improvement,* his wife always retorts, but she doesn't mean it. She's got a sense of humour. She has to, he guesses, to survive being married to him.

They reach the end of the corridor and he presses the button on the wall. His gaze flickers over the prisoner's handcuffs, just to make sure they're still on. A uniformed man in a small glass box beyond looks up at them and buzzes the lock, and they nod at him and walk through, and downstairs, towards the interview room.

"I fantasise about moments like this, you know," says the convict, while they are alone in the stairwell.

"Shut up, Staedler."

"Really, I do. I lie awake and—"

"I said shut your mouth, prisoner," says the guard. "Or I'll shut it for you."

The interview room is clean and quiet, an island of calm deep inside the churning nest that is the rest of the prison. The guard shoves the con towards a chair. "Sit."

"Why, thank you," Staedler says. "I believe I will."

The chair scrapes the floor: fingernails on a chalkboard.

The prisoner shakes his silver cuffs at the guard. "Can you take these off?"

124

The guard ignores him.

"I want to make a good impression," says Staedler.

"No," says the guard.

"No, you won't take them off, or no, it's impossible for me to make a good impression?"

"Both."

"You have a real gift for conversation, you know that, Gerber? You're a regular raconteur."

"It was her condition," says the guard.

"Er, what now?"

"The reason you have to keep the cuffs on. It was one of her conditions. For visiting you."

Michael Staedler chokes on a short, bitter laugh.

"It's not like ... it's not like I would *hurt* her. Why would I hurt her? That would be really stupid."

"Ja, well. What can I say?" says Gerber. "She knows what you're in here for."


On cue, there is a gentle knock on the half-ajar door.

"Gentlemen?" she says. She's exceptionally beautiful with her chestnut skin and shining eyes. Kohl-lined lids and glossy hair, recently cut. She's a welcome sight after a double shift. The guard's nose twitches. He can smell her hand cream—coconut—and something else.

Anxiety?

Staedler shoots up. "You're even more beautiful than your profile picture."

Suhana Vallabh takes a deep breath and moves to the other side of the room. She places her dictaphone on the table, as well as her notebook, and a cheap ballpoint pen.

"You've seen my profile picture?" she asks. "You've been doing your homework."

Staedler laughs. "Yes."

"Well," says Suhana. "I have, too." She's not laughing.

"I guess ... I guess that's what makes you so good at your job," he says.

"And how would you know that I am good at my job?"

He scratches his cheek. "You've won awards, right?"

"Some."

"You've been promoted three times in five years. They say you'll be the chief editor at the National Trib in no time."

"I doubt it. It's a desk job. I wouldn't be able to do a desk job."

"Ah," says Michael. "You like the action."

"If that's what you call this."

"What would *you* call it?"

They both sit down, and the guard relaxes his grip on his baton; allows his muscles to loosen up.

"You tell me," says Suhana. "You're the one who's been calling me five times a day for a month--"

"Six weeks."

"*You're* the one who has been harassing *me*, so you tell me, Mister Staedler. You tell me what it is we're doing here."

"Isn't it obvious?" he asks.

"In my job it pays to not jump to conclusions."

"That's good. I like that."

"What are you so intent on getting from me?"

Staedler stretches his arms, then places his hands on his head. "I'm sensing some hostility."

"Damn right, I'm hostile."

"But aren't you supposed to be ... you know ... cool?"

"Cool?"

"Professional," he says. "Impartial."

They glare at each other for a moment.

"Look," the prisoner says. "I'm not sure this is going to work. If you already have a problem with me. I don't think the article will ... come out right."

"What did you expect? You imagined I'd come in here and be ... what? *Friendly* to you?"

"I don't see why not. You could at least be ... polite."

"Polite? To a murderer?"

"Attempted. It was *attempted* murder."

Suhana stares him down.

"This is really not going how I planned..."

"I will not be manipulated by a narcissistic creep like you."

"Now, hold on a minute."

"Look at me," she says, and waits for him to do so. "I am not a supporting actor in your sick reality. Got it?"

"I've got it. I've got it."

"Now," she says, opening her notebook and scraping it flat on the table. "Let's begin."

～

SIX MONTHS EARLIER

The lecturer tells the punchline of his Kubrick-Spielberg joke and the hall rings with laughter. The bell sounds, and the students pack their bags.

"Argh. Kubrick's my least favourite director in this syllabus," says the blonde girl sitting a seat away from Michael. She stands up and slings her bag over her shoulder, ready to leave.

"Er..." he says.

"What?" asks the girl. "Do you, like, *get* his work?"

Michael's cheeks flush; perspiration prickles his skin.

Her arms fall to her sides. "Please tell me you like his work and that you can explain him to me?"

Her eyes are wide, blue, clear. *Eyes to drown in,* thinks Michael.

"Well," he says. "Yes?"

Her eyes grow wider still. "Yes?"

"I'm a bit of a fan," he says.

*Obsessed* would be more accurate, but he didn't want to come across as a weirdo.

"I have all his films. And a projector. You can borrow my external drive, if you like."

"Oh my god, thank you!"

"Or," he says, heart thrumming. "If you like, we can ... we can watch them together and I'll talk you through them."

"Really?! You'd do that for me?" Her face is a beacon.

He looks down at the floor. "I wouldn't mind."

"I'm Jessica," she says.

*I know,* he thinks. They exchange numbers and walk out, together.

Jessica sighs in relief. "Oh my goodness, how lucky am I?"

"Sorry?"

"Out of all these students, I chose to sit next to *you!*"

*No, you didn't,* he thinks. *I'm the one who found you.*

~

PRESENT DAY

. . .

129

"So you met in university," says Suhana. "Film school."

She constantly takes notes. Her rushed scribbling, pen on page, is like a persistent whisper in the room.

"It was perfect," Staedler says. He looks smug, as if he's lying in a hammock somewhere on a tropical island instead of here, at a dented metal table in handcuffs.

"So Miss Sears just happened to sit next to you in that class."

"Well," says Mike, and laughs. "Not quite."

"You engineered it?"

"You make it sound so cold. Calculated."

Suhana chews on the back of her pen. Michael imagines the inner tube bursting, and black ink bleeding onto the journalist's lips and tongue; pictures a stream of it running down her chin.

"How did you do it?" she asks.

"I ... overheard her ... in an earlier lecture."

"So you were following her, before?"

"Not 'following' her. I would sit behind her in class. I liked watching the back of her head."

"You liked the ... back of her head?"

He laughs again. "Obviously I liked the front of her head better. But I didn't want to freak her out. I stayed under the radar until—"

"Until you were ready to make contact."

"I overheard her talking to a friend—Sam—about how she was dreading the Kubrick assignment. How she didn't 'get' him and avoided watching his films ... and now she was behind and was worried that she wouldn't be able to catch up."

"So you downloaded all his movies."

"No, I really did have all his films on my drive."

"But you made sure you sat next to her in that particular class. The Kubrick class."

He rubs at a dirty mark on the knee of his orange overalls. "Yes."

"God," says the journalist. "My blood just ran cold."

Michael looks up at her. "Well, it worked, didn't it?"


"So you coached her? You watched movies together."

"Yes. We started with Kubrick and then moved on to Hitchcock and Scorsese. Tim Burton, Woody Allen. It wasn't just Kubrick they needed help with."

"They?"

"Jess and her friend, Sam. Sam was convenient to have around."

"How so?"

"It meant that I could spend long, glorious hours with Jessica without it getting weird."

"Weird?"

"You know. Awkward."

"It removed the romantic aspect from your time together."

"For her."

"And for you?"

"I was in love with her before she even knew I existed."

SIX MONTHS EARLIER

"I'm so glad we're here," bubbles Jessica. "I've been waiting for this movie to come out for ages!"

"Hey, Mike," says Sam. "Do you want popcorn?"

"Ugh. No, thank you."

Jessica laughs. "Mike hates popcorn."

"Hates popcorn?" says Sam. "Who hates *popcorn?* You're weird, Mike."

"What can I say? It's not the first time I've been called 'weird'."

"It's because he's a movie snob," says Jessica. "The popcorn thing. He can't stand it when he's trying to focus on the narrative arc of a film and everyone around him is crunching corn right in his ear. It's like, no one even thinks about it, they just order it automatically. And then they eat it automatically. Like robots. Or zombies."

"Popcorn zombies," says Michael, and Jessica laughs out loud.

"Finally!" he says.

Jessica looks at him. "What?"

He gazes at her for just a split-second too long.

"Finally, I've found a woman who understands me."

PRESENT DAY

"So you were pretending to tutor them—"

"No," says Mike, shaking his head. "I really was tutoring them."

"But actually it was a guise to spend time with Miss Sears."

"I thought if we spent enough time together she'd see that we were meant to be together. She'd see that we were the perfect pair. A couple of swans. Do you know that swans mate for life?"

Suhana ignores his question. "You thought she'd fall in love with you."

"Yes. That's how it goes, you know? The tropes for a romance film. Guy meets girl. Guy and girl fall in love. There's a bit of conflict to get through but then they always end up together. Usually at an airport, where he has to run to catch her before it's too late. And then there's the HEA."

"HEA?"

"Happily Ever After. It's not a true romance if there's no happy ending."

"In Hollywood, maybe. But Jessica didn't return your feelings."

"It was discouraging, sometimes. But I knew if I just kept going, she would see the light. See the light of my love."

"If you 'kept going'?"

"You know," Mike shrugs. "If I kept at it. Kept helping her. Kept wooing her. Kept charming her."

"You thought you were charming?"

"I can be charming. I was always on my best behaviour with her."

"Hm," says Suhana, writing in her book.

"What?"

"Did your 'best behaviour' include ... you know ... what happened, in the end?"

"That was different."

"Why?"

"That wasn't me. I mean, that's not what I'm usually like."

Suhana shakes her head. "I disagree. I think that person you were—in the end—that was the *real* you. The charming thing is just a mask."

"No."

"That person who abducted Miss Sears. Who tried to kill her. I think *that* is the real Michael Staedler."

"No, that's not true. I'm a good guy. I'm usually a good guy."

"That's what stalkers always say. That's what psychopaths say. They think they're normal. Because they can't see the menace in their behaviour. They can't see it for what it really is."

"I'm not a psychopath. I have empathy. I know right from wrong."

"Do you?"

"I know it was wrong. What I ... did to Jess."

"Let me guess: you never meant to hurt her," says Suhana.

He gives her a pointed look. She's not playing along.

Suhana taps her page. "You're wasting my time."

"What do you want me to say? I'm being honest."

"Are you?" They stare at each other over the grey table. "Let's skip the bullshit. Let's get to the real story. The real bloody beating heart of it."

Michael sits back, looks down at wrists where the cuffs have rasped his skin.

"When did it start to go wrong?"

Staedler scratches his cheek again. "I replay it over and over in my head like ... it's like watching dailies."

"Dailies? What do you mean?"

"It's like, when you're watching your daily film rushes. What you got that day, uncut, unedited. Take after take after take of the same scene. Identical, apart from the most subtle differences. Then, if you're not happy with it, you can re-shoot, the next day. But ..."

"But life isn't like that," says Suhana.

Staedler gazes at her. "I guess this prison would be empty if life was like that."

SIX MONTHS EARLIER

. . .

"Put that camera away, Mike," says Jessica, swatting at him.

She's sitting at her dormitory desk, going over her study notes, and the soundtrack to a Kubrick film is playing in the background.

"Not until you give me what I want," he says.

"What?"

"Just look into the camera. I just need a glance."

Jessica glares at him.

"There we go. Got it. You're so bloody beautiful. You're my leading lady."

"Cut it out, Mike. I'm being serious. Switch that camera off."

Michael puts the camera down, but it's still recording.

"There! It's down. I've put it down."

"I wish you wouldn't do that," says Jessica. "I hate it."

"But you're so ... Jess, you're so beautiful. We need to share it with the world."

"What? Shut up."

"I mean it."

Annoyed, she frowns at her watch. "Where's Sam? She's late. We need to start."

"Sam's not coming."

"Yes, she is."

"She's not," says Mike. "I texted her earlier. I told her we're meeting tomorrow. Instead of today."

PRESENT DAY

"So you told her how you felt about her," says Suhana.

"It was a mistake."

"But she knew, anyway."

"Ja. I guess she did. It was like ... It was like I was on fire, inside, when I was near her. She must have felt that. The furnace of my desire. Felt something."

"You made a pass at her, and she said she didn't want to see you anymore."

"Yes."

"But you were still in the same class?"

"It was a good excuse to bump into her."

"How did she react?"

"Cold shoulder."

"She didn't kick up a fuss?"

"Not in class. Not in the beginning. But when I couldn't get her to look at me in class, I had to get creative."

"You started following her around campus."

"Don't say it like that. Don't say it like I was a lovesick puppy."

"Weren't you?"

"You make me sound pathetic."

"Hm."

"Yes. I would follow her. I'd sit at the table next to hers in the canteen and watch her eat."

"Why?"

"Why? Because I was in love with her!"

Suhana puts down her pen and crosses her arms. "Mister Staedler. What do you think 'love' is?

"It's impossible to put into words."

"Try."

He sighs and kicks the legs of his chair with the heel of his boot.

"I had this feeling. Like I could never be complete without her. Like there was no point in living if I couldn't have her. Like at one pole there is Jessica and light and happiness and at the other pole there is just ... nothing. Darkness. Depression. A vacuum where my heart should be. I wanted to wake up with her and cook breakfast for her, spoil her. Hold her. They were good, noble feelings. I wanted to care for her, not harm her."

"But you did."

"Harm her?"

"Are you in denial about that?"

"No. But it was never ... it was never my intention. All I really want to do is take care of her. It's just ... unfortunate, how things worked out.

. . .

Suhana reaches forward and grabs two bottles of water. She twists off the cap and gives one to Staedler.

"I want to go back to ... your definition of love."

Michael gulps the water down. "What's the point?"

"I'm still trying to understand what happened."

"Thank you."

"I'm sure you're thirsty."

"I mean, for trying to understand. I'm not a monster, you know. Despite what everyone has been saying."

"What has everyone been saying?"

"That I'm a psycho. A murderer. I'm not. Things just—"

"Yes?"

"Things just got out of hand. Spiralled out of control."

"But you *did* try to kill her?"

Staedler puts the empty bottle on the table. He doesn't answer.

"I can see that you haven't accepted it yet. Accepted what you have done."

"I have."

"You still think that you're a good guy!"

"I am!"

Suhana laughs bitterly.

"You don't get it," he says.

"Why don't you explain it to me? Isn't that why we're here?"

"It's like this: I was in love with Jessica, right?"

"Yes."

"Full-blown, over-the-top, mad, intense, obsessional love, right?"

Suhana blinks at him. "Right."

"So, think of it this way: If she felt the same way — if she returned my feelings — then we would have this amazingly beautiful thing, right? Obsessional love is celebrated the world over. Romeo and Juliet. Tristan and Isolde. Brangelina. It's the ultimate human experience."

"Yes," says Suhana, picking up her pen again.

"It's this beautiful thing. Right?"

"Yes, but—"

"Hear me out. So love is seen as this wonderful thing. But only when it is returned! That doesn't make any sense. It's not fair."

"How so?"

"As soon as love is unrequited it is all of a sudden transformed into something bad. Something shameful."

"Alright," says the journalist.

"So you understand?"

"I understand what you're saying. I get your point. It's valid."

Staedler slams the table with his fists, making her and the prison guard jump. "Thank you!" he says.

"And I understand how you need to see yourself as a good guy, even when—"

"Even when I'm sitting here in handcuffs."

"Yes," says Suhana.

"Look, it's not like I don't understand what I did was wrong."

"But you keep making excuses for your behaviour."

"Well, there were circumstances that ... complicated the situation."

Suhana taps her fingers on the table. "You mean the restraining order."

∼

SIX MONTHS EARLIER

The university security guard grips Staedler's arm and knocks on the Head of Arts Department's office door.

"Hi, Prof," he says.

A handsome woman wearing bifocals on the tip of her nose looks up at them. "Oh!" she says. "What have we here?"

"Staedler," says the guard.

She pauses to think. "Who?"

"Michael Staedler. The one with the restraining order."

Mike's mouth hangs open. "What?! What restraining order? Bullshit!"

"I showed him the university's suspension letter, but he wouldn't leave. Tried to run for it."

"You can't suspend me," he says. "I haven't done anything wrong."

The professor searches her desk for a piece of paper. "Have you been harassing a fellow student?"

"Of course not!"

"Okay, let's put it this way: have you been sending Miss Sears flowers? Love letters? Hiding the letters in her personal belongings?"

"Yes! Since when are flowers and love letters cause for being kicked out of university?"

"Have you been phoning and texting her repeatedly?"

"Yes."

She stops searching her desk and looks at him. "Yes?"

"That's what friends do!"

"Do friends also follow each other around? Even off campus?"

"That was a coincidence."

"Really?"

"The film. I bumped into Jessica at the cinema. We're both film students. It's the cinema closest to campus. It's bound to happen."

"And you just happened to sit in the seat right behind her in this film?"

Staedler stares at her, mouth clamped shut.

"I know it wasn't a coincidence, Mister Staedler, because it wasn't the first time you did it. Sears reported that you had done the same thing on two separate occasions prior to this incident. She can't go to the cinema any more. This is far from ideal. As you said, she's a film student."

"It's not like I was *doing* anything to her. I was just there to watch the movies. I'm allowed to, you know. The last time I checked, this was a free country. I have rights."

"Jessica can't go to the cinema anymore. She can't go to class. She can't even eat lunch on campus because you're always there, watching her."

"Of course I'm here. It's my university, too! What would you have me do? Skip class?"

"That's exactly what I need you to do. Hence the suspension, which will be in place for as long as the restraining order is valid." She finds it and holds it up to him. "My advice to you is to move on quickly."

"Move on? Leave my life behind? She's just overreacting!"

"No, Mister Staedler," the professor says, pushing her glasses up the bridge of her nose. "I don't think she is."

## PRESENT DAY

"So," says Suhana. "You got kicked out of varsity."

"Suspended. Till further notice."

"You think it was worth it?"

"What?"

"Your one-sided love affair. Was it worth losing everything you'd worked for at school? It says in my file that you were the top student in the whole arts department for three years running."

"It would have been worth it, if it had worked."

"If what had worked?"

"If she had ... if we had gotten together. Then everything would have been more than worth it."

"You're a very determined person."

"Yes. I have focus. Determination. It's supposed to be a good thing. It was always a good thing until I met Jessica."

"Do you know why I can tell you right now that she isn't the right person for you?"

"Why?"

"Because when you're in love, in a healthy, robust relationship— you bring out the best in one another."

"Hm."

"While I think ... I think that Sears brought out the worst in you."

"That's ... difficult to hear."

"Because it's true."

"I mean, all light has a shadow."

"Can you explain that?"

"I mean, she's like, all light. So there are bound to be shadows."

"I'm not sure I follow. Are you the shadow?"

"Only when I'm around her."

~

FIVE MONTHS EARLIER

Michael's face is tinted blue from the screen in front of him. His finger clicks on his mouse automatically, as if it's a separate, robotic part of his body. The curtains are closed and the room is dark. He rewinds and plays, rewinds and plays while he edits his film. Jessica looks more beautiful than ever.

*Put that camera away, Mike.*

*Put that camera away.*

*Not until you give me what I want.*

*Give me what I want.*

*Give me what I want.*

*You're my leading lady.*

*Put that camera away, Mike.*

*You're my leading lady.*

*You're a really good guy.*

*I'm very fond of you.*

*Mike.*

*You're a really good guy.*

*I'm very fond of you.*

*I'm not attracted to you. In that way.*

*I'm ... attracted to you. In that way.*

The doorbell rings, snapping Michael out of his trance. It rings twice more before he gets to the front door. When he opens it, the sunlight burns his eyes. He sees a police uniform.

"Michael Staedler?"

Michael frowns. "Yes?"

"We need to have a word."

"You're cops?"

"Looks like we've got a clever one." His name badge says Thebe.

"I just ... I don't understand why you're here."

"Well, we'll explain it to you," say the other one. Moletse.

Staedler hesitates.

"Don't worry," says Thebe. "We'll talk slowly."

The officers push past him and he follows them into his lounge.

"You're going to tell me why you're here?"

"I think you know why we're here."

Michael's face starts to sweat. "I didn't go near her, if that's why."

"Really?" asks Thebe.

"Really."

Moletse steps forward. "We have a witness who says she saw you across the road from where Miss Sears was having coffee with a friend. You were filming her again."

"A witness?"

"The friend. The friend is the witness. Samantha Brodkey."

"Well," says Michael. "I wasn't breaking the law. I wasn't within fifty metres of her."

Thebe looks around the lounge. "Very clever, hey?"

Moletse nods. "Do you know what they do with clever people in prison?"

Michael snorts with laughter. "Prison?"

"You laugh, *wena,* but I know your type."

"Really?" says Staedler. "What's that?"

"Rich, white, educated."

"Arrogant," chips in Moletse.

"You think you're out of reach of the law. But you're not."

"I didn't break the law," says Michael.

"You *almost* broke the law. We're here to tell you that we're watching you."

"We've got our eyes on you, Staedler," says Moletse. "Consider this a friendly warning."

Thebe doesn't take his eyes off Michael. "A pretty whitey like you, in prison ... they won't *almost* break you."

~

PRESENT DAY

The prison guard eyes Suhana; he's had enough of Staedler's voice and wants to go home to his family. She looks at her watch and sees she has ten minutes left of the interview.

"Why did you keep filming her?" she asks.

"She was my leading lady."

"You were ... making a film about her?"

"I've made a film about her."

"You know that's just another form of harassment? Filming people without their consent?"

"When I couldn't have Jessica ... and I couldn't go to class ... the film became my project. I became obsessed with it. Obsessed with making it beautiful."

"Something like that," says Suhana, "stolen from someone ... can never be beautiful."

"I spent hundreds of hours on it. Cutting and layering and adding sound. I worked on it every waking moment, till it was perfect. Until it was absolutely perfect."

"And then something happened."

"Jessica dropped out of class and left the country," says Staedler.

"How did you know?"

"Tumblr. She was tagged in a photo at the airport. It was a British Airways counter. I guessed that she was flying to the UK. She had a big suitcase—bigger than a holiday suitcase."

"That's a lot of information from one shot."

"In film school they say that a picture is worth a thousand words. We're trained to dissect visuals. In a really tight film there are no extraneous details. Everything in the frame is there for a reason. Everything in that photo: the BA logo, the bag, the clothes she was wearing ... they all told me one thing."

"What was that?"

"That I needed to go to her."

FOUR MONTHS EARLIER

DONEGAL, IRELAND


Mike runs past an electric green hedge and shops with old clay roof-tiles. The fading pink light tints the buildings with a romantic blush, and the copper fixtures turn to gold. He sees his reflection in his peripheral vision in the shiny glass shopfronts. There are a handful of pedestrians, a couple of cars, but it's quiet enough, and Jessica is so close he can smell her.

He reaches her and touches the soft padding of her jacket.

"Jessica!" he says.

She spins around, shocked, as if his hand had carried an electric current. "No," she says, frowning. "It can't be."

Michael laughs. "I tracked you down! It wasn't easy. You covered your tracks well but I refused to give up."

Jessica looks around, ready to scream for help. But he wasn't doing anything to her, wasn't threatening her. "How?"

"I'll tell you everything over coffee! Let's go in here."

His hard grip burns her elbow. He tries to steer her into the café.

"Mike," she says, trying to find the right words. "I have a restraining order against you."

"I'm not angry about that. I've forgiven you. Anyway, things have changed."

She wrenches her arm away from him. "Nothing has changed!"

He looks up and down the street and then directly into her eyes. They used to make him think of the ocean but now the wide blue irises irritate him. "Don't cause a fuss again. I flew all the way out here to talk to you!"

"I am here to get away from you!" she shouts at him. "I left my whole life behind to get rid of you!"

"This is our airport scene," says Michael, gesturing at the setting sun and the lush trees. "And it's perfect."

Jess starts walking away from him, but he grabs her arm again. She cries out. A pedestrian in a brown suit walks past but doesn't stop.

"Jess," he says, his jaw muscles tight with tension. "It's time for our happy ending."

Jessica takes off, but Michael grabs her and shoves her into a side alley; the wall is dark with lichen and damp. She starts to scream for help but he forces his hand over her mouth and whispers into her ear.

"Don't scream. Don't scream. Be quiet. Jess, just be quiet."

She stops flailing and screaming, but she can't stop the terrified moans that force their way out of her. Michael directs her along the shop alleyway, and takes her phone out from her jacket pocket.

"Now, I told you. I have something to show you. I came all the way here to show this to you. The least you can do is watch it with me."

Michael wrestles her towards his hired car, and opens the back door. Jessica fights, spraying fine gravel as she tries to kick him, tries to break his grip. She bites down on his hand, and he snaps, slamming her into the side of the car. While she is stunned, he pushes her onto the backseat, zips a cable-tie around her wrists and slams the door, then jumps in the driver's seat and locks all the doors. There is silence in the confined space, apart from their heavy breathing. Staedler brings his hand up to look at it and sees it's bleeding, then frowns at her in the rearview mirror.

"I can't believe I have you in my car. It's like ... it's like I'm dreaming. You have no idea how happy you have just made me."

Jessica blows her hair out of her face. "What are you going to do to me?"

Michael starts the car. Jessica notices paraphernalia on the floor. Cable ties, rope, video camera.

"What are all these things for? What are they?"

"Oh, don't worry about those things. We won't need them if you don't do anything silly."

He puts the car into reverse and backs out of the bay. "You'll see. There's really nothing to worry about."

Michael clicks 'play' on the car sound system. It's the Kubrik soundtrack from that day in her dorm when she swatted him away.

"You see?" he says. "I've planned every last detail. I even made a playlist for you. It's full of our songs."

Jessica can't help the tears. They stream down her cheeks.

"Hey!" he says, gently. "Don't be upset! Please don't cry! I am going to take such good care of you.

They pull up to a small cabin in the forest, which glows against the pines painted black by the night. Michael throws Jessica over his shoulder and carries her up the path. Just before they reach the door, he stops and takes a deep breath of the forest air.

"I won't tell anyone what you've done," says Jessica. "Just let me go and no one has to know anything."

"No, my love," he says. "It's too late for that."

Jessica whimpers softly. Michael opens the cabin door and puts her down inside, locking the door behind them.

"You see?" he says. "It's perfect. Our own private cinema!"

Jessica looks around for windows wide enough to squeeze through. There are none.

"I brought my projector," he says. "And my own cotton bed sheet from home because you never know, do you? I mean, you never know what colour the sheets will be, in a small cabin in an Irish forest."

"What will we watch?"

"Isn't it obvious?"

Jessica gulps and shakes her head; spilt mascara patterns her cheeks.

"We'll watch my film!" he says. "My film about us."


Michael walks to the kitchen and struggles to open a drawer. He pulls out a large knife and brings it over to Jessica, then cuts her cable tie off with it and pushes her down, onto the couch.

He places the knife on the side table and picks up the projector remote, presses 'play'. After the title sequence plays out, the establishing shot shocks Jessica.

"That's my bedroom," she says.

"Yes."

"How did you get that shot?"

"What do you mean?"

"You were there? In my *bedroom*? How did you—"

"You know me. How dedicated I am. It wasn't ideal—I mean, the angle—as you can see. But I made it work."

It cuts to Jessica under a tree, Jessica eating lunch with a friend, Jessica in class. There are jump-cuts to close-ups of her face, her eyes begging him to stop. You hear her edited voiceover:

*Mike.*

*You're a really good guy.*

*I'm very fond of you.*

*Mike.*

*I'm … attracted to you. In that way.*

Jessica shoots up. "I can't watch this."

"What? Why? It's beautiful. And I made it for you."

She roars and tears down the cotton sheet, kicks the projector over so that it crashes and breaks on the floor.

"Hey!" Michael shouts at her. "Stop that! Stop!"

She slams his laptop shut, picks it up, and throws it at him as hard as she can. He dodges it and it explodes on the floor.

"I hate it!" she shouts. "You hear me? I hate your film."

"You don't … you don't mean that."

"It's the *ugliest* thing I've ever seen!"

"Don't say that!"

"It's disgusting! You disgust me!"

Staedler lashes out, punching her to keep her quiet. She reels backwards, but doesn't fall. Her hands fly up to her face and come away bloody.

"We will *never be together*. You understand? *Never!*"

Michael launches his whole body at her, slamming her to the ground. Her head cracks on the floor and the world starts to look grey; her hair is immediately wet with shining crimson. She sticks her fingers into his eyes and he yells, then she bucks him off her and lunges for the knife. Her fingers are slippery with blood but she manages to grab it. She can feel herself losing consciousness, but forces herself to stay awake, even though it feels like all her blood has drained out of her. Michael slams into her again but this time she turns towards him just in time, and he uses his own strength to impale himself on the knife she's holding in front of her heart.

He gurgles and falls onto the cold stone cabin floor, and Jessica loses consciousness and collapses down next to him, into his widely splayed arms. A police car siren sounds in the distance.

∾

PRESENT DAY

Michael opens his prison overalls and lifts his white shirt beneath it. The scar is still fresh, and it repulses Suhana.

"How did they find you?" she asks.

He drops his shirt. "As soon as I grabbed her, in town, Jess pressed her panic button on her phone. It was in her jacket pocket."

"How does that work?"

"It's just an app. If you're in trouble you hit a button on the phone and it sends a message to the local authorities. Then they can track your movements."

"Clever."

Staedler puts his fists on the table. "If I had just … If I had just taken her phone earlier."

The journalist narrows her eyes at him. "Did you hear what you just said?"

"What?"

"Surely, Staedler," she laughs despite the seriousness of the situation. "Surely if you have one regret, it's not that you didn't take her phone earlier."

"Oh, I know what you mean. "

"Do you?"

"Ja, my regret should be that I took her in the first place. Or … that I even *met* her in the first place."

"That's why I think you're really not sorry at all."

"Of course I'm sorry," he says.

"You're not sorry for what you've done. You're only sorry you got caught."

"What *you* still don't understand is that Jessica Sears is the love of my life."

Suhana sighs and drums her fingers on her knee.

"Don't you see that it's impossible for me to *regret* having met her?" he says.

"You wouldn't change ... being in here? Sitting here with handcuffs on?"

"Not if it meant never having met her. This is *real* love. Real love is not brittle. It doesn't break under pressure."

The prison guard uncrosses his arms and pointedly looks at his watch.

Suhana nods at him. "So why am I here, then?"

Staedler laughs; it's an ugly sound. "You thought that I asked you here to express my regret to the public? To issue a message of unconditional apology? To say that I have seen the error in my ways?"

"Yes. I did. That's why I came."

He laughs again. "No."

Something clicks in Suhana's head. "I'm not going to give Miss Sears any kind of message for you, if that is what you're trying to do."

"That's not why I asked you to come," he says.

"Okay people," says the guard. "Time's up. Visiting hours are over."

· · ·

Suhana gathers her things, and stands up, scraping her chair. The sound scratches at her frayed nerves.

Michael jumps up. "Wait!"

The prison guard takes a step forward, one hand towards Staedler, one hand hovering over his Beretta. "You sit down, prisoner!"

"But—"

"You sit down!"

Staedler lowers himself into his chair, desperation sponging the blood from his face. "Please," he says.

"Make it quick, Staedler. You've wasted enough of my time." Suhana grips her notebook in her clammy hand.

"I wanted to promote the film," he says.

She glares at him. "You what?"

"I thought Jess and I could spend a romantic weekend in the cabin together while the world thought that I had kidnapped her. I'd upload the video and ... well, with that kind of coverage ... everyone would watch the film!"

"While the world *thought* that you had kidnapped her?"

"Yes! I was going to tell her the plan, that day, but then she started to run away."

Suhana takes a step towards the door.

"That's where you come in," he says. "Because of the ... complications ... I wasn't able to share the link to the film on my website. And I don't have online privileges here—"

"You're not serious."

"All I need you to do is share the link."

He hands her a scrap of paper with a URL printed neatly on it.

"I'm sure it'll go viral in no time."


Suhana folds the scrap of paper into her notebook and closes it, and presses stop on her dictaphone. The guard opens the door for her, and she walks out of the interview room. He watches her for a moment, angry that she's been manipulated, but then he sees her drop the notebook into a wire mesh bin, half-full with used polystyrene cups and chip packets, and keep walking.


The guard smirks and hoists the prisoner up from out of his chair. He'll walk Staedler back to his cell and that will be the end of his double-shift. He's looking forward to getting home to his wife and kids. He feels the photo of them pulse in his badge wallet. He'll be able to report to his wife that he got through one more day of not having his face rearranged, and if she's in a good mood, she'll laugh.

∾

## 10

## MEMORY, MIRRORS, AND THE WORLD
## INSIDE MY HEAD

I ANSWER TO SANDRA, but that's not my real name.

That's what's written on my birth certificate. I know because I keep it in my collection drawer along with the other Curiosities. I stole it when I was a child and my parents never noticed.

Growing up was a bad time. I don't remember the details but one day there was a birthday party and a yellow cake, and Mom said that I *changed*; that my behaviour *shifted*. They never took responsibility for the early childhood trauma, and I don't have any memories of it, so their maleficence remains unpunished.

What I do remember is their everyday viciousness which scraped away at the consciousness of what could have been a healthy little girl. I was born physically fit, as far as I can tell, but abuse has a way of peeling your skin away, and then your flesh, until there is nothing left but pink stained bones. I have to keep building the layers back. A crazy quilt of mismatching patches sewn together with snapped-off sinews, red cotton, and copper wire. Some days I feel as if I have my original skin back, but mostly the breeze is cold against my raw flesh and shining stitches.

One of the problems with not having your original skin intact is that other people can smell your vulnerability. School was a venue of vultures. The childbirds would sniff out my exposed parts and peck, peck, peck, undoing all my work, unspooling me, until my skeleton was close to showing and I had to hide away: the class store-room, a bathroom stall, or the janitor's cleaning supply cupboard where I was once locked in, overnight. Dark-panic-bleach. My palms, bruised and bleeding from hammering on the door, still ache with the memory. My hands were swollen and shredded, but what hurt the most is that no one came looking for me.

I didn't have company until I was eleven, when Silke and Froggo joined me. We shared the same reality, and had a tele-pathic connection. We could hear each other's thoughts and feel each other's emotions. Kind of like imaginary friends, I guess, except that they were more real and immediate to me than anyone else in the Outside World. They were certainly more tactile than my parents, who just ghosted in and out of our rundown house. Just because Silke and Froggo were 'in my head' didn't make them any less tangible. If you've ever had referred pain, you'll know what I mean. But this was the shinier side of the coin: referred protection.

. . .

After a few years, Silke and Froggo faded away to make space for the second generation of Alters. This time there were twenty-eight alternate personalities, and together we created the World Inside My Head (Wimh). Wimh is 0.46 the size of earth and has over three million people on it. As you can imagine, it takes a lot of work to maintain. Mieke, Lapis, Ruth, Stracky and I were the main creators. We made everything from the claw-root velvet grass, to the gold-flecked purple sunsets, to the 206-ward smart-hospitals in every city. We dyed the oceans green and created animals from scratch. At first it was a complete mess, with trees growing out of trucks and fish swimming on roof-tiles, but slowly we carved and moulded and spray-painted until everything was ship-shape and shiny.

The people in this world—we call them the Inhabs—are made in every culture you can imagine, and every tint of skin. They all lead complex lives. The population skews towards female—as most of my Alters are female—and homosexuality is the norm. 'Straight' means gay in Wimh, and 'Queer' means hetero. We didn't set out to make it like this (not consciously, anyway) but we are happy with it and it works very well. Most of the time the Inhabs take care of themselves, but because there are so many of them they do require constant monitoring and inter-vention.

We watch them as closely as we can, and busy ourselves, like Gods, turning the volume dial on the weather up and down and around (it's a spherical dial, like a planet scored with ancient symbols). The weather dial has its own orbit, but we have to keep an eye on it. Sometimes it's sensitive to the energy that surrounds it—like when I'm having an argument with someone in the Outside World—and tries to turn on extreme weather.

We try to keep Wimh mild and safe, so hurricanes and snow-storms are best avoided.

The political situation takes a lot more time to manage, but that is a whole story on its own. Think of when you had to cram all those essays into your head before your final history exam. Now imagine all those events are real and happening right now, on your watch, in your world. It's a lot more work than twenty-nine personalities can manage, but we try our best. We triage the current events and respond to emergencies first. All this while I'm trying to deal with my Outside life: getting to the dentist, meeting my targets at work, laughing at my husband's jokes, paying off my mortgage, changing a tyre in the rain. It takes a lot of energy, and a lot of focus. I used to live in fear of getting really sick, because I know what would happen if I took my hands off the wheel. Let's just say the weather dial would be the least of our problems.

But getting sick wasn't what I should have been afraid of; being too trusting was.

One of the boldest Alters, Ruth, got power-hungry and tried to become the Primary personality. This became known as The Betrayal. She did this by distracting me with an overactive volcano on the Isle of Sarkon in the east Thalassa ocean. The volcano had been threatening to erupt for weeks but we were too busy preventing a civil war in Rustacia and saving the seed-back whales who seemed intent on beaching themselves on the rocky Amalinia coastline. Also, the presidentess of the south-western quadrant of the globe ordered her army to attack the people of the south-eastern quad and seize their land, and we had to intervene before too many children were killed. There aren't that many children in Wimh and they need to be protected. We don't like armies or wars, but that's what happens when you leave the Inhabs up to their own devices for too long.

So Ruth directed my attention towards the Sarkon volcano and while I was trying to cool it down and evacuate the Inhabs at the same time, she made her move for power, and killed every other Alter, save for three that she didn't reach in time. She called a secret emergency meeting without my knowledge, telling the others that it was my wish to announce something important, and when they were all in the Control Room she ran her Samurai sword though every one of them, slicing them in half in one whirl. The three Alters who were late for the meeting saw what happened, locked her in, and rushed to tell me. I had to leave work early and sit in a café, drinking tea while tears streamed down my face, absorbing what had happened and figuring out what had to be done.

I was devastated. The Betrayal hurt me very deeply; it felt as if I had that same silver sword forced in through my own ribcage. Sometimes I still feel it there, wedged in between my stomach and my heart. I felt like one of those beached whales dying slowly on the cold, wet sand, with only black rocks for pillows. Worst of all was the realisation that Ruth was too powerful to sustain, so I had to cut her off from my consciousness completely. But you can't just choose one Alter to slice out of your life. It's all or nothing, so I had to say goodbye to the survivors, too. I had to burn down the Control Room and edit out the innocent survivors, which just made that razor-edged blade burn more.

For the first time in years, my head was silent.

As if the leaden heartache wasn't enough to deal with, I had to run the whole of Wimh on my own. A world that took a team of twenty-nine Alters to run now fell on my shoulders alone.

Sometimes I'd stay awake all night just to work my way through the dangerous events on the horizon. It's hard to get to sleep, anyway, when you know that bad things are happening and only you can prevent them. I can't sleep when I know that children are in danger. Those all-nighters were sometimes a welcome event, because I had time to myself to just sit in the dark and drink bottomless coffee and I could be really productive and race through those near-catastrophes, preventing as much tragedy as I could.

Even though I'd be really tired the next day and my co-workers would talk behind my back and joke that I must be moonlighting, at least I knew that I'd staved off the worst for the day, and I could have a small measure of calm. My colleagues weren't as bad as the childbirds; they didn't go for exposed flesh. Instead they just chirped and fluttered around me. Not vultures now but watercooler wagtails.

My husband, Eric, started worrying about me, and I didn't like that. *Sandra,* he said, *Sandra,* even though he knows that's not my real name. *Sandra, please, don't get lost.* I started fainting at work, and worried about falling asleep while driving home in the evenings.

I know what you're thinking. You're thinking I should have just let Wimh devolve into chaos to save my own Outside life. But it doesn't work like that. Wimh is a permanent structure in my mind, one that I can never stop managing. The World Inside My Head keeps my mind fused, so losing it is never an option. If one's body unspooling seems bad, know that one's mind unspooling is far, far worse. Wimh is my mental version of the crazy quilt that keeps my body together. My brain is sewn up with warm copper wire.

I tell Eric that I don't want children, which is a lie. I'd love to have two children, a boy and a girl. A pigeon pair. But the hard truth is that I'd never be able to cope. I'm responsible for the wellbeing of three million, six hundred, and forty-seven people (and counting). If I added my own baby to the mix it would be asking for trouble. What if she fell off a swing and knocked out a tooth? I'd lose my grip on Wimh for as long as it would take me to stop her screaming, mop up the blood, and get her to casualty. Hundreds of Inhabs might die for that milk tooth. Milk Tooth Massacre. Like anyone who grew up lonely, craving a happy home, I would so love to have children, but it's just not a risk I can afford to take.

Without help, Wimh was spinning out of control and I could feel myself burning out. I remember not being able to keep my scratchy eyes open but trying to force them, trying to conjure alertness from a numb slab of a brain that had nothing left to give. Then there were men in white coats, and Eric by my side. An IV line and delicious days of slumber while hundreds of Inhabs died, slaughtered as I slept. There was nothing I could do; the drugs kept me under.

Just in time, the third generation of Alters arrived, and these are the people I live with today. Lexi, Belladonna, Snowden, Jaqueline and Harriet (Harry) showed up first, and others followed, slowly filling all the empty positions left by Ruth's terrible deed. One of my favourite Alters is a four-year-old girl called Lamb Chop.

The third generation is different to the previous ones. They live with me, but they also live as Inhabs on Wimh. They are Alter-Inhabs. They are Inhabs who have somehow elevated themselves to live in our collective hivemind. It's a strange limbo to navigate, but we do our best to accept things as they are.

The Alter-Inhabs don't languish in my head while I get on with doing the laundry and filling out my time sheets at work. They have incredibly complex lives of their own, existing in the world I created and strive so hard to maintain. We share memories and experiences, and I know them just as well as they know me. Through them I have lived almost a hundred lives. I lived through utter heartbreak when Harry's lover, Saldegard, was shot in an alley and left to die in a dirty puddle of rainwater. But I also lived through Saldegard's death as I was with her when she was murdered for that amulet she was never supposed to wear. I can still taste that water, flavoured with a rainbow petrol surface sheen and under-shoe muck. That wasn't the first time I've been killed.

I've been pushed off a cliff in Eires before (Eires is like Ireland but covered with lichen and overrun with skinny pigs and grey-billed ducks). It was during a lover's quarrel. I still have a small scar on my head, under my hair, where the jagged rock cracked open my skull like a robin's egg. Technically it was Sinead's skull, but as I'm sure you're beginning to understand, it was my skull, too. I never sought revenge. I have too much to do, and I've been told that Sinead's lover/murderess has become ill with the guilt of it. Some kind of skin malady that keeps her isolated in her turf-roofed warren, with only tarantulas for company.

I was also killed in the Farsea earthquake I was trying to prevent. I was pregnant then (Lexi was with child) and dying that day did upset me. Looking back, it's probably why I succumbed: because I was being pulled between being God and being Lexi and my power and focus was divided. Instead of trying to stop the earthquake, which would take one hundred percent of my attention, I was trying to save Lexi and our baby's life by getting her out of danger. There was a shelter nearby that I thought we may just make it to in time, but then the earth underneath us yawned and a giant crevasse appeared and we were dancing in the air, and the next thing our feet touched was the carpet of death.

I've died a lot, but I've also lived a lot. People call me Sandra but I've had a lot of names. I've had countless careers and scores of lovers. I've been male, female, young, old, ugly, beautiful. I've been a warrior, an explorer, a teacher. Most importantly, I've experienced every single human emotion that exists. This is why I would never get rid of Wimh, even if I could. It enriches my mundane Outside life beyond explanation.

Sometimes I stick my head up in our open-plan office at work and see everyone tapping away at their keyboards and I just think, how can this be your only life? How can you not get deeply depressed and bored with your monochromatic existence that you don't just jump out of the staffroom window into the city traffic below?

You know when some people say they have lived a thousand lives through the books they've read? Well, imagine that in 3D: living, breathing, gasping. Touching textures that come alive beneath your fingertips. Blood rushing, lungs billowing, pupils dilating. The steaming scent of past lives smoking through every otherwise mundane moment. Some people call what I have a disorder, but more than anything, I see it as a gift, and I can't imagine living any other way.

It's not without its challenges, of course. Multiple memory losses are common, but luckily my Alters are here to fill me in. This is imperative to give the impression to others that I am living a 'normal' life. Without my Alters telling me in snippets what I've forgotten I wouldn't be able to hold down my job, wouldn't be able to have a decent dinner-time conversation with Eric or do the grocery shopping. Coping means, in part, listening to the Alters, and the rest is guessing and smoothing over the Lost Time, which I have become proficient at. Still, sometimes there are chinks, and all I can hope for is that people will forgive me and move on.

Memory is one of our challenges, and so are mirrors. The problem with mirrors is that they are ubiquitous, and that they make the Alters unhappy. It's a difficult thing, catching sight of your reflection, and the face staring back at you is not your own. You'd think it's something you'd get used to, but you don't. For example, Thando is a tall, handsome woman with dark mahogany skin, and braids down to her waist. She wears the cultural dress and red-earth make-up of the Zimbilo people. She's a beautiful and proud woman. When she is with me (i.e. sharing my body in co-conciousness) and we get into the elevator at work—which is a surreal painting of floor-to-ceiling mirrors—our reflection is thrust into our vision, and Thando gets very upset. I'm a medium-height white woman with chapped lips and mousy hair who has never had the time or inclination to follow fashion. I can feel Thando's alarm. They don't complain about it, but I can feel their inward cries of despair. Their anguish is my anguish, so now we take the stairs.

Living this way is not easy, but for me, personally, the advantages far outweigh the challenges. To be so alone and isolated as a child, to be pecked apart and have to constantly sew up my skin, and then to bloom into this life of camaraderie at every turn: always someone to share an interesting idea with, express a feeling. Always someone to hold my hand, to touch my forehead when I am feeling unwell, to guide me to bed when I say I'm too busy to rest.

· · ·

These small things that are, in fact, everything.

When people in the Outside World learn about my situation they often ask why I don't seek therapy, and my reply is: why should I mend something that isn't broken? I've done my research. Therapy would mean attempting to integrate the various alternate personalities, which sounds like a disaster waiting to happen. We are all too different. You just need to compare our handwriting to see that. Also, I'd have to go back to running Wimh on my own, which didn't go very well last time. Anyway, wouldn't the integration be the same as what Ruth did to us? Wouldn't it be like killing the other Alters to seize the throne? I'll never betray them like that. We are bound by necessity and honour. They protect me, and I protect them.

I'm not power-hungry, but I am the god of my own world, and I'm not going to allow a psychologist to change that. I know more about my state of mind than any doctor ever will. Maybe therapy would mean trying to coax Sandra out of her permanent hibernation, seeing as she is the original owner of this body.

I don't think that would be good for any of us.

≈

# 11

# BLACKWATER ESTUARY

MALDON COUNTY, ESSEX, 1579 AD

POPPY RUNS through the nettles and mud. Her boots threaten to betray her by sticking to the mire. She has, in her basket, the fruits of her morning's foraging: rosemary blossoms, clove stalks and resin of myhrr. She's tempted to abandon the harvest but thinks that the plants might come in handy for what's ahead, so she firms her grasp on the handle and keeps running. Above her, the ravens cry.

Thomas, the bearded dairy man, greets her and she raises a hand in acknowledgement. Her neighbour, Picot, does the same. She smells the ale on him as she passes. She can tell that he wants her to stop, wants a chat, but she doesn't have time. She is needed at her homestead.

The hand-painted wooden sign on her gate says Elderberry Farm, but it's not a farm, not really. It's a modest plot with just enough land to keep her pantry well-stocked and her neighbours sweet with gifts and good bartering. As the village herbalist and honey-keeper, she's known to have the greenest fingers in Maldon county.

Poppy jogs past the town square. The tradespeople are packing up their wares for the day: spun cloth; tallow candles; lavender soap; crusty loaves of rye. She'll bake her own bread in the morning. She prefers a finer grind to what the bakers here sell. You have to be careful of telling people that kind of thing though. You have to buy a loaf of theirs every now and then just to show that you don't think yourself better than them. Poppy doesn't care much about what people think, but she also knows that it's the tallest flowers that get scythed.

At last she reaches her dirt track: the Osgoods, the Middletons, the Giffords and then she bursts through her gate and scrambles into the hall. She can't see her Jacqueline anywhere. Her cat skitters out of her way.

"Poppy!" shouts a man with his hat in his white-knuckled hands. "You're here!"

Lily, his wife, is bent over and groaning.

"Did Jacquie find you? We sent her to find you."

The ravens had sounded the alarm, pulled her from the forest. But that is not for the Glovers to know.

Poppy is perspiring; breathing hard. She moves over to Goodwife Glover and takes her hands.

"Lily. Is it bad?"

"There's something wrong," says the woman, her face as pale as a waning moon. "I can feel it. There's something wrong."

"She's in pain," offers Glover.

"Thank you," says Poppy, "I'll take over now."

The man looks relieved as she leads his lowing wife away. A labour chamber is no place for a man.

There is a welcoming coolness of the stone floors but this won't last long: the fireplace is stocked with wood and kindling, ready to come alive at the flick of a flint. Poppy fills her black kettle with well water and hangs it over the straw, which she lights. She flings off her hat, smoothes her wisps down and scrubs her hands. People scoff at this habit, but she believes that clean hands are an outward symbol of a clean mind and she needs to keep her wits about her if this is going to be a difficult birth.

"When did they start?"

"This morning," says Lily, "but they were easy."

Poppy opens all the lattice windows and drawers, unties all the knots.

"You should have come over."

She gives Lily a Jasper gemstone to hold.

"I didn't want to bother you too soon. I was timing them. But then —" she grinds her teeth, "But then something changed."

"Climb on the birthing stool. Let me take a look."

"Poppy," she says, desperate, grabbing Poppy's wrist. "I don't want the baby to die."

"The baby won't die." Poppy begins rubbing salve on Lily's tightening belly. Perhaps what Lily also meant was, 'I don't want to die'. But that she cannot guarantee.

Three hours later, just as Goodwife Glover's screams threaten to strip the straw from the very roof, just as Poppy is deciding that she will have to cut the baby out, there is a change; a shift. The breeze picks up outside and whistles its news. There is to be a concession for this woman, and, surely enough, the screeching subsides and a waxy grey head appears. One more exhausted push from Lily is enough to deliver him in his entirety, despite his generous size. The baby is limp and blue and isn't taking a breath. Poppy rubs him vigorously with a cloth, trying to wake him up. She smacks his sides, pokes his ribs, speaks to him sternly, telling him it's time to wake up, but the baby does not stir. The women make sad eye contact. Lily is too exhausted to cry.

Poppy lays him on the bed, pinches his nostrils closed and uses her own breath to inflate the boy's lungs. On her third exhalation he starts. He gurgles and coughs. Poppy clears his mouth and breathes into him again and this time he takes the next breath himself and rewards the women with a yell of indignation.

Poppy, lightheaded with relief, cuts his cord at four fingers and wraps him up in swaddling cloth, lays him on Lily's chest, plugs his mouth with his mother's nipple. What happened? What changed the almost certain outcome that this baby would not live? She cleans up while the newborn suckles, then bathes him in salt and honey to dry up his humors and comfort his limbs, all the while sending up a prayer of thanks to the forces that let this be.

When Glover comes to collect his wife and son he is buoyant with gratitude. He bundles them out into the night and into his cart, which he has lined with fresh linen for the occasion. He pays Poppy in cotton shifts and salted meat and she can tell that he wishes he could give her more. Just before he instructs the horse to trot, Lily stops him, and takes a ribbon from around her neck.

"Take this," she says, pressing it into Poppy's palm. "It was my mother's and her mother's before her."

"I can't."

"Take it. You saved my boy's life. I want you to have it."

Poppy opens her hand. A silver amulet knotted onto the ribbon shines in the starlight. The face of a wolf.

"It's Fenrir," Lily whispers, "the Wolf God." But Poppy knows that already.


Jacqueline had arrived home while the birth was in progress and put herself to bed. She is an independent child. She has to be, with her father gone and the hours that Poppy works. She sits on the edge of her seven-year-old's bed, near the purring cat who lifts her sleepy head in greeting. Poppy strokes Jacqueline's cheek, her chin, marvelling at the beautiful creature sleeping before her; marvelling at the terrible love she feels for this being. Still a baby, really, despite her brave appearance and her sword-fighting skills.

Poppy will need her help tomorrow. She's behind on the preserving and pickling of the late harvest and she doesn't like to see one ear of wheat wasted. Jacquie will complain, saying she has a village to conquer — she's going through a Viking phase — but she'll do her chores first. She always does.

There's a knock on the door. The first thing that comes to mind is the Glover baby. Has something happened? Has he fallen asleep and not woken up? She makes her way to the front of the house and pulls open the door.

The fire is fading, so a naked Poppy slides out of her thistledown bed to add more coal. Her braids are undone, her dark hair drifts down her back. Devereaux watches her move in the firelight.

"God, you're something," he growls. "Come back here, you vixen."

"Not a vixen," says Poppy, moving towards him.

He takes her hands. "No?"

She leans towards him, puts his hands on her breasts. Shows him the amulet on her chest. "A wolf."

"Ah," he says, and howls like a homesick hound.

"Shush! Shush!" she says, laughing, covering his mouth. "You'll wake Applejack."

He stops howling, sucks her finger instead.

"You're delicious. Tell me again why you won't come and live with me?"

"Stop it," says Poppy. "You know that's impossible, with your... status."

"Since when do you care what people think?"

"It's not that."

"I could hire you. You could live in the house under the guise of proper employment."

"And what? Become your concubine?"

"My staff are discreet."

She shoots him a look of dubiety. "No thank you."

"It would be a luxurious life, compared to this, anyway."

"I'm very happy here, thank you very much, in this humble hovel."

"I didn't mean that. You wouldn't have to worry about money. You wouldn't have to work. You could save these lovely fingers of yours."

Poppy laughs. Not work? She shakes her head. It wouldn't be her life.

There is a glint in Devereaux's eye. He's angry.

"It's because of him, isn't it?"

He's always had a quick temper, this pale, high-cheekboned man. He was spoilt as a child is Poppy's guess. Never wanted for anything. As beautiful as a god, but blighted all the same.

"It's because of that bastard."

"Don't call him that. He's my husband."

"Husband?" He laughs without humour. "Richard left you five years ago."

"He's still my husband."

He raises his voice. "You think he'll come back, but he won't."

Poppy knows she should stop the argument, soothe Devereaux with words and caresses, but she's had a long day and is not in the mood for supplication.

"You don't know that."

"You don't even know if he's alive!"

"He's Applejack's father."

"He doesn't give a damn about Applejack."

"Watch your words Devereaux."

"You still love him. You're a fool!" He smashes his pewter goblet on the floor. It clangs against the stone and rolls to a stop.

"I think you should leave."

Devereaux sets his jaw and begins pulling his breeches on.

"And this time... this time, I don't think you should come back."

He puts on his doublet.

"You don't mean that."

"I do. You want to control me and I will not be controlled."

She knows she is playing with fire. He grabs his jerkin off the nearby stool sending the chair cracking to the floor. Shakes it onto his shoulders. He grabs her arm roughly, takes one last hard look at her. She can tell that he wants to strike her. Bruise her. He wants to see her cry.

"You'll be sorry," he says, his irises black with fury. He squeezes her jaw so hard her teeth cut into the inside of her cheek.

She unclamps his grip, returns his solid gaze, although she is shaking inside. The taste of copper is in her mouth. "Goodbye, Devereaux."

Poppy is tending the bees when the Justice of the Peace arrives.

The honey yield has been especially good since she's been experimenting with dog roses and wild raspberry. Jacqueline comes to call her. Her lips, hands and apron are spattered with crimson and it makes for a macabre sight.

"Have you finished with the beetroot?" she asks her daughter, patting her head and twirling a loose strand of fringe.

"Yes, Mama."

"Good girl." She looks at the officer, then back at Applejack. "Go and wash up, and then you can play."

"But I haven't yet —"

"It's all right," she says. "Take a break. We'll carry on this afternoon."

Applejack hesitates, then whirls away.

Poppy shields her eyes from the morning sun. "Good day, Valance," she says, and he tips his hat to her. "Is there something you're needing? More oak tincture for your wife, perhaps? I have some at the ready."

Valance looks uncomfortable. He shifts his weight from foot to foot. "We've had another complaint."

Poppy sighs, crosses her arms. "What is it, this time?"

"Picot. He says that you've hexed his milk cow."

"Will you... will you say that again?"

"His cow. When he retired last night the cow was in perfect health. This morning it won't stand up."

"And how does this have anything to do with me?"

"He says you had an argument last week."

"It was hardly an argument. He owes me money and I reminded him it was overdue."

"He says you cursed the cow for revenge."

"That's ridiculous. Picot is poor and he wants my land. He's always had his eye on it."

"That may be. But, as I said, it's not the first complaint. And your neighbour is not the only one asserting that —"

"Asserting what?"

"Asserting that you've made a deal with the Devil."

Poppy laughs out loud. "The Devil?" she says. "How does one go about doing something like that?"

Valance lifts and lowers his shoulders. His whole body is a shrug. Poppy feels like striking some sense into his barrel chest.

"You spend too much time in the forest," he says.

"I'm a herbalist."

"And you know that the forest is where the evil spirits convene."

"Nonsense."

"In the woods. The Robbins boy saw you... dancing. Speaking in tongues."

"That boy is troubled. He is always watching me. He stalks me wherever I go."

"You were angry. You chased him away."

"I'm always chasing him away. He's menacing."

"When you were angry with him a storm brewed."

"Did it? I don't remember."

"It killed the dog. The Robbins's dog."

"What is the charge, exactly? Do you believe I killed a dog?"

"I'm not sure what to believe. But —"

"You know that I am a good woman, Valance."

"You don't come to church as often as you used to."

"I work this land on my own. I treat sick people. I birth babies. I don't always have time for Pastor Thurlowe's ramblings."

"It's that kind of thing," says Valance, sucking his teeth. "It's saying that kind of thing that gets you into trouble. You read too much."

"So I'll be on trial for dancing in the woods and reading too much?"

"We'll begin at four. In the town hall."

"An inquisition?"

"An examination. You have to answer to the allegations. That's the way it is."

"But they're ridiculous."

"That's the way it is."

The town hall is packed by half-three. Poppy has never realised how many people want to see her undone until she walks into the humming, high-roofed room. There is a ripple of quiet as she steps through the threshold. The Justice of the Peace catches a glimpse of her and is relieved. He doesn't want to be forced to arrest her. The timber boards creak under her as she moves towards the front of the room where the pulpit serves as a makeshift witness box. Pastor Thurlowe looks on intently. He has, Poppy is certain, been waiting patiently for this day to come. She looks out into the gathering, seeing men she had saved from the Sweating Sickness, women whose hands she had held through labour, the very children she helped deliver now bouncing on their laps.

"Poppy Gossard, you stand accused," says Valance, "of forming a pact with the Devil. Of naughty dealings, and, ultimately, of witchcraft."

The crowd murmurs. Poppy's hands are white fists. There is a buzz and a snap in the room as if there is a storm cloud above them.

"Willard Picot. Please come forward and make your case against the accused."

Poppy's neighbour, sober for once, comes up to address Valance. He tells the story of how he oftentimes sees strange happenings at Poppy's home. He smells her potions brewing, hears her cry out at night in pain and ecstasy as she indulges in sexual relations with the devil. Bawdy comments escape the gallery. Pastor Thurlowe's ears turn red and burn at the idea.

"And how do you know, sir, that it's the presence of the devil that you observe?"

"Depraved fornication." Spittle gathers at the sides of his mouth. "If you were to hear it, Justice, you would know it, too."

"No wonder her husband left her!" shouts someone from the gallery.

"She's had her fair share of company since then," says another onlooker.

Picot speaks slowly and deliberately as if he has rehearsed his story. He tells of their argument over his debt, and of how his milk cow is still too ill to stand. "I'll wager right now," he says, "that if I were to pay her the money she's so intent on, my cow would recover forthwith. Otherwise, I don't think she'll make it through the night."

"Do it, then," cries a lout from the gallery. "Pay her and we'll see."

Picot is known for his poverty. The little money he has always seems to find its way to the ale house. When Poppy had sold him the scouring sand he needed she hadn't been expecting a hasty return.

Picot shoots a look at Valance and Valance agrees. "Pay her, Picot and we'll see."

The man pulls out his leather purse and counts out some bronze coins. He counts them twice, then hands them over to Valance, who deposits them into Poppy's clammy palm. Where, she wonders, did he get this money?

"We'll listen to the other witnesses then make our way to Picot's holding."

Other witnesses? Who else will betray her today?

Goodwife Kemp takes the stand. Tells of how her summer crop of rye spoiled before it was harvested. Under questioning, she reveals that she saw Poppy Gossard's striped cat amongst the stalks, rubbing its cheeks on the green of the produce. Six days later the plants were infected with a mould that drooped their crowns and rotted their grains. Bent, crooked, blighted.

"Goodie Kemp," says Valance, "do you contend that the Gossard cat is capable of evil deeds?"

"A cat is a cat," sniffs Kemp. "I afford no special powers to them unless they are bewitched."

"Bewitched?"

"Every person in Maldon County knows that Gossard is a sorceress and that that creature is her familiar."

A low moan emerges from the gallery. Some people toss their heads. Poppy frowns at them, trying to establish the mood of their judgement. Kemp is excused. The crowd waits.

"I request the testimony now of Goodwife Glover," says Valance.

Thank God. A friend.

Lily limps, baby bundled in her arms and sighs in her direction. Poppy can smell the rose oil on the baby's skin. She tells the court of her difficult birth.

"He wasn't breathing," she tells the Justice. "He wasn't moving. His skin was saxe. But Poppy... Poppy brought him back to life." The baby fusses and she rocks him to comfort him.

Pastor Thurlowe cannot sit still any longer. He stands up, bringing the court to attention. He seems genuinely shocked by the testimony. "Brought him back to life? Are we to believe that you gave birth to a dead baby and this woman summoned his spirit to live?"

"I didn't mean —"

"How did she do it?" Thurlowe asks. "Was there a tincture? An incantation?"

"No, no, pastor. All I mean is that I think, with a less experienced midwife, Baby Glover wouldn't be here today."

"How did she do it, woman? Tell us!"

"I was almost delirious with pain. Exhaustion. I may not be a dependable witness."

"Tell us what you saw," says Valance. He is gentle with her.

"She held him up, scolded him, smacked him."

"She struck a newborn infant?" asks Thurlowe, eager to show his astonishment to the gallery.

"It's not an uncommon practice," says Lily. "A man wouldn't know, of course, of the happenings in a labour chamber."

"Go on," says Valance.

"He still wouldn't wake. And by then I was sure that he would not."

"Then what did she do?"

"She... she put her lips to his. She used her own breath to wake him up."

The pastor seems at once horrified and joyous. "Are you saying that this woman, Poppy Gossard, breathed life into your dead infant?"

There is silence in the hall. Lily seems unsure of how to answer. She looks at Poppy, then searches for her husband's face in the gallery.

"Goodie Glover," says Valance, "Is it true?"

"That's not how it was. Or, it's not what you think. It was a miracle. A wondrous gift."

"Blasphemy!" shouts Thurlowe. "Human beings are not capable of miracle-making. Only the Good Lord Himself can do such a thing."

"Perhaps the Good Lord used Poppy as his instrument," says Lily, eyes brimming.

"More like the Devil," says Thurlowe. "The Devil's instrument. The Devil. The Devil. The Devil."

Lily shields her baby from the pastor, as if his words create a sinister splatter about him.

"There was no evil-doing in that room," she urges, looking desperate now to leave the stand, but the pastor won't allow it.

"You said yourself that you are an unreliable witness to the event. You were barely conscious and Gossard took advantage of your vulnerability."

The people buzz with anticipation.

"That's not the truth," says Lily.

Poppy stands. "This is nothing but scandalmongering. I will not be slandered in this way."

Valance steps forward with his hands out. "Good people, please," but the pastor is in full swing. He struts as if on a stage.

"I put it to the good people of Maldon County that Poppy Gossard is a powerful witch, guilty of general *maleficium* and of harmful sorcery against her neighbours."

A roar reverberates from the back of the court. People stand and jeer. Poppy can't tell if they are in her favour or against her.

Valance offers his hand to Lily, helps her down off the stand and leads her to her husband, who stands, nonplussed, just outside the commotion.

"She's a good woman, Valance." He takes Poppy's trembling hand. "You know she is."

"Picot's cow will decide the matter," says the Justice. "We'll be on our way there now."

It's a twenty-minute walk from the town hall to Picot's place and Picot leads the way even though everyone knows exactly where he lives. They walk over a dark patch of hardened sand, stained by the blood of a bear recently baited there and ripped apart by dogs. Picot side-eyes Poppy. Guilt shines from his face. Valance walks beside his charge. Poppy is unsure if he's there to protect her or to keep her from escaping. Where would she go?

They reach the blackjack lane which snakes up to Picot's ramshackle house. The townspeople, their target now in view, hurry past the weeds, tripping on the pink stones. Poppy lifts her woollen shift to avoid the unlucky seeds. Picot, still sober, is surprisingly agile as he strides up to his plot. Before Poppy catches sight of the cow she knows it is dead. Her neighbour wails and curses.

"She killed it!" he shouts, pointing a dirty finger at Poppy. "She killed my cow."

The people gather around the poor animal, belly distended by death fumes, bluebottle flies for eyelashes.

"You said that if the animal recovered it would be proof of my magick," says Poppy. "You can't have it both ways."

"You tricked us," says Picot. "Of course you would not allow the cow to recover if it would be evidence of your evildoing."

"So whether the cow lived or died it would be proof of my witchcraft?"

"You're not called cunning folk for nought."

"I've had enough of this eyewash," says Poppy. "I've honest work to do." She begins walking towards her house, mere metres away, but a strong grip on her arm holds her back.

"I think we need to get back to the inquest," says Valance.

"It was an examination. Now it's an inquest?"

"Now it's a trial."

The Robbins boy comes running up, face afluster. "There's no time for a trial," he says. His breathing is short and sour.

"What do you mean, son?"

"Her magick is too strong. She's already taken revenge all over town."

"Gossard has been in my company all hours today. She's had no time to make mischief."

"Her familiars carry out her demonry for her. I've seen it with my own eyes."

"Your imagination is the thing of demons, lad," says Poppy, "not my work."

The boy ignores her, licks his lips. "It's true. I saw that cat of hers, black and oily as tar slipping into Goodie Kemp's yard and attacking one of her hens. The fowl is dead. As dead as this cow."

A voice from the gathering, "I saw that devil cat go into the house of the Glovers."

The people titter in fright.

Valance turns from Poppy to the boy. "For what? What now?"

"To murder the baby, of course," splutters the boy. "The unbaptised baby. She's taking revenge on all the witnesses who testified today. And when she's finished with them, you will all be next."

Valance seems alarmed.

"That cat," the Robbins boy says, "I'm going to tie that cat in a sack and drown it in the river."

Poppy slaps the boy hard across the face. The onlookers gasp and back away from her.

"Shut your mouth, vermin," hisses Poppy. "Don't you see how dangerous your game is?"

"It's no game," he shouts, rubbing his cheek. "I've seen this witch in the forest, communing with Satan."

"I've also seen her," says Beckett, the cobbler, "coming out of the woods at all hours with her herbs and poisons."

"And me," says Ellis.

"And me," says Landsdowne. "And I've seen her talk to animals."

"She'll kill that Glover baby if we let her."

"Where is Goodwife Glover? Someone must fetch her. Warn her."

"I think we have all the proof we need," comes a voice from the back of the gathering. The people part and Pastor Thurlowe walks towards Poppy and Valance. "Raise your eyes to the tree-tops. Do you see the ravens gathered?"

The people look up, and indeed, the uppermost branches are host to scores of black birds.

"There is evil in our midst," says Thurlowe. "It is imperative that we exorcise it before more harm is done."

Townspeople prod Poppy in her back forcing her back towards the town square. Thurlowe clutches his Bible and recites verse. She tries to break away from them but Landsdowne brings rough twine to tie her hands behind her back and Ellis threatens to put a sack over her head. Jacqueline comes running, but the villagers keep her away.

"Ma!" she screams, "Ma!"

Poppy thrashes at her captors to get to Jacqueline. She's almost able to touch Jacquie's hand, the soft, hot hands she knows so well, but they pull her back into their marching circle. Poppy's wrists chafe and bleed. She tries to escape again and again and the people become angered by her perseverance. Beckett strikes her to quieten her spirit. Every attempt to get to Jacquie now is met with a hammering to her face or a kick to her stomach. By the time they reach town she can no longer hear well and her face is dripping with blood. Her daughter's screams are dull in the distance. Her dress is torn and she has lost her shoes.

The old gallow-tree is grey in the shade of the triangular tower of the church. Tired sunlight, the colour of orange preserve, washes the top half of the surrounding buildings. Poppy is led up the stairs by Valance, who loses his grip on her for a moment. His hands tremble. The executioner stands alongside pastor Thurlowe, who is crimson-faced and still spouting verse like a madman. The bearded hangman readies the noose for her, but the pastor stops him.

"The mercy of the Lord insists I give you one last chance," he says.

Poppy's eyes search for her daughter in the crowd. Faces, angry and shocked, stare back. People she has shared her modest harvests with, given honey gifts, baked bread for, mixed medicine. Children she has minded, babies she has delivered. She wants to believe this is not really happening, but her mind and heart are so wide awake that she knows this is no night terror. The noose is real. She can smell the barley breath of the hangman.

"One last chance," says the hell-faced pastor, "to confess your sins and give your life to the Lord."

"I am innocent of the crimes you are so eager to lay upon me," says Poppy. "I have done no wrong."

She sees Devereaux on the steps of the town hall. He won't look in her direction. She wants to call out to him for help. Can't he see what is happening here? Surely with his money and influence he can help her? But then she sees him exchange a few words with Picot and Picot swills from a new cup and then Poppy understands.

"Confess!" the pastor shouts into her face.

"I have nothing to confess."

"Allow the Lord God to show you mercy, child."

"I will not beg for forgiveness for something I have not done."

A blue calm settles over Poppy. A resignation. A knowledge that this is what has to happen.

"Do you think I see not the evil in your body?"

"Any evil you see in my body is in your mind alone."

"Confess!" he shouts again.

"*You* are the wicked one," Poppy says and spits in his face.

Thurlowe lifts a hand as if to strike her, but she does not flinch. His eyes are mean coal-sparks.

"This Satan-worshipper before you," he says to the crowd, wiping his face, "this blackened soul is past redemption."

Cries of assent echo from the crowd. The hangman steps forward again, places the noose around Poppy's neck and tightens it. She battles to breathe. The pastor stops him as before. "Stop," he says and struggles to loosen it.

The crowd is silenced. Valance looks on, clearly hoping for a reprieve. Thurlowe puts his hand on Poppy's shoulder.

"A noose is not enough," he says. "We need to exorcise the very demons that inhabit her being."

The executioner seems unsure what to do. Valance starts to argue but a look from the pastor cuts him down.

"Fire," says Thurlowe, "Only fire will purge the wicked spirit of this woman."

A cry goes up from the onlookers. The Robbins boy is already depositing twigs and other kindling beneath the tumble-down timber platform. Thurlowe helps the hangman lash Poppy to the hanging post.

"Exodus 22 verse 18. Thou shalt not suffer a witch to live," he says to her as he trusses her with a dirty cord. "Thou shalt not suffer a witch to live."

The fire has been lit. Poppy can feel the sneaking warmth on her bruised soles, can smell the smoke. She finally catches sight of Jacqueline who is screaming and flailing below.

"Take her away," shouts Poppy, her voice hoarse. "I beg of you, do not let her witness this."

Her legs are starting to burn. She feels warm liquid, like tea, wet her shift. She looks down and sees that her bladder has emptied. Thurlowe is rigid, one arm pointing up to salute his imagined heaven, the fingers of the other hand on his brow, eyes closed, as he mutters his own incantations. A raven swoops down like an arrow and pecks at his eyelid, scratching his cheek. He waves it away and finds blood on his cheekbone.

"Ma! Ma!" cries the girl, still a baby. Still her precious baby. Poppy tries to reach out to her but her arms are firmly bound in place. The fire is gathering momentum. Her dress catches the flame.

"Please," cries Poppy to the crowd. "Please take my Applejack away." She sees the baker's face, the hay-man, the seamstress - all cold and unmoving as winter cliffs. She tries to ask again but she cannot breathe for the smoke. No one heeds her but then Glover breaks through the crowd, calling out and clapping at the people. In his wake, Lily Glover, babe in arms, pushes forward and grabs Jacquie's arm and leads her away.

Poppy can hardly hear or see; the heat is agony. Her skin blisters and pops. Her mind begins drifting to a higher place. She sees the Robbins boy pick-pocketing the gawping onlookers. The pain becomes unendurable. More ravens come, perching on railings and barrels and abandoned market-stalls. Soon the air is black with their squawking and feather-litter.

Glover is bellowing. "Help her, help her," he is shouting, "she burns too slowly."

Suddenly people are spurred into action as if woken from a trance and they gather whatever fuel they can and add it to the bonfire beneath her. There is light and darkness and no air to breathe, and a huge explosion barbed with stars. Poppy sees peach blossoms and lavender and bees and Applejack as a toddler; dimples; clouds; soil. Stars sparkle before her and at last, at last the torment fades, at first into black, then grey, then white.

## 12

# PERKY PILGRIM

**Trip Advisor Review: Bridge Gate. 1 out of 5 stars.**

Being the intrepid traveller that I am, I have not been afraid to occasionally "rough it". Subsequently, I have stayed in a few dastardly places in my life, but this one takes the cake. And I used the term 'cake' as an idiomatic expression, as there is certainly no cake to be found here. No sponge puddings, no pastries, and certainly no scones. Tea time here is an affront to everything that is good and right in the world.

As my dear Aunt Daphne used to say: "The mind, she boggles, Señor."

My goodness, where to start? I feel overwhelmed by the sheer scope of the indignities I have endured inside these four walls, painted the colour of day-old gruel. It's a shameful, shameful establishment. Even though it's no secret that I am an accomplished writer, I am finding it difficult to write this review. But as Winston Churchill once said: "This is no time for ease and comfort. It is time to dare and endure." So I shall try my best. Tally ho!

Here are my complaints so far:

The mattresses are old and thin and the springs poke you in the spleen if you let them. The bedding is abrasive on the naked skin and smells of boiled cabbage.

The previously mentioned walls are grimy and graffitied. I try my best to not read the scrawled profanities at the risk of being transported back to my childhood nightmares when I would be trapped in a public school restroom stall. The walls also seem to close in each day. Now, I know this is not possible, but sometimes when I lie on the bed and stare at the ceiling, I have the sensation that the room is getting smaller and smaller. Perhaps a fresh coat of paint would assist in this regard, ideally a bright, cheerful colour that does not remind one of getting one's face smashed into one's boarding school porridge.

The toilet has no seat, nor a lid, and there is seldom any toilet tissue. You would think that toilet tissue would be ubiquitous in a place with so many arses around but I'm afraid this is not the case. Now I did hesitate to mention the disgraceful ablution facilities, as I don't want to lower the general tone of my reviews, but it is also my duty to inform you, dear reader, so I'm afraid it has come down to this. There is no cistern handle to speak of, and the pipes are often blocked, which causes the bowl to over-flow. I don't have to tell you that on those days, it's an abysmal state of affairs, especially when your room-mate suffers from protracted bouts of irritable bowel syndrome. It doesn't bear thinking about, but think about it we must, as we cannot ignore the cascading lake of toilet water that has become as much a feature of this room as the small square window above our heads that taunts us with its view of the crisp blue sky, just beyond our reach.

Talking about arses, my room-mate is a thoroughly awful man (named 'Smith' of all things)—a mad man, really—who likes to think of himself as a philosopher. The tripe that man speaks ... well, let's just say, it whiffs of our room's unique water feature. As if these accommodations are not torturous enough without having to listen to a man who quite clearly received his "PHD" from a lucky dip cereal box. (!)

And speaking of cereal ... Oh, reader. I know I complained about the bland, touristy "paella" at that hotel in Ibiza—where the staff all rudely spoke Spanish—and the "make-your-own-pasta" at Coconut Bungalows, but I have hit a dangerous new low here. Despite my sophisticated palate I won't hesitate to tell you that I can handle pedestrian fare. I was, after all, brought up on stale bread, tinned bean soup, and brown apples. There is a time and a place for simple food, and this does not offend me. However, please believe me when I tell you that the slop that is served here is beyond any kind of redemption. The food is never warm, despite lying under the heat lamps in the canteen, attracting all manner of bacteria. We are offered bread-rolls like rocks, powdered scrambled eggs that bounce if you drop them, congealed oats that turn to cement the moment they hit your stomach. And that is just breakfast! Don't get me started on lunches or dinners, or the infamous "chicken stew" that looks neon green on our blue melamine plates. Oh, it pains me, body and soul. Body, especially, and it's made clear on a daily basis that the same is true for Smith.

I find the staff here incredibly rude. They seem to be, without exception, muscle-bound brutes who grunt commands and expect us to obey. I have tried to educate the man who services my room, but all he does is smirk in an unkind way.

As I always try to round off my reviews on a positive note, I will tell you about the magnificent garden outside, which is the highlight of my day, every day. There is a man here, Locklear, who keeps to himself and tends the grounds. His rose garden, in particular, is an absolute beauty to behold. It reminds me so of my beloved Aunt Daphne, who used to prune her roses to within an inch of their lives. But sometimes wounds are transformative: the cruelty paid off, and we were rewarded with a swathe of blooms in Summer. The petals of silk and the profusion of scent, well! A florescence of a well-maintained rose garden can rouse even the most weary of spirits.

Signing off with a reluctant one star. Reluctant because this "establishment" deserves far less, but I have just returned from a walk in the gardens and it has made me feel overly generous.

Sincerely,

Alan Perkins

Dear Mr Perkins

While I appreciate your review of Bridge Gate, I must hasten to remind you that this establishment is not a B&B, and while you are incarcerated here it may serve you well to remember that. The prison guards are not your "staff", and I would refrain from criticising the food served in the mess hall. If the head cook, Danté, gets wind of you insulting his cooking ... well, let's just say there may be certain bodily fluids splashed into your next bowl of oats, and they won't be tears.

I'd also caution you against speaking badly about fellow inmates on a public forum like this. If you continue to disparage your peers, or the prison itself, I will have no choice but to remove your library (and hence your online) privileges.

I appreciate your co-operation in this regard.

Frederick Collis

Director at Bridge Gate Prison

Department of Correctional Services

## Trip Advisor Review: Bridge Gate. 2 out of 5 stars.

Well! I am happy to say that after leaving the original review, things around here have been improving. Just knowing that I have the Director's ear makes a significant difference to my state of mind. Sometimes, in the hospitality business, it's enough to simply *listen* to your customers. But Mr Collis went one further than that ... the toilet has been fixed! It still has no lid, or seat, (or handle!) but the pipes have been unblocked and it no longer floods the room with water that smells of doom and regret.

Acting on Mr Collis's advice, I introduced myself to the head cook—although I must admit I did find it difficult to not chuckle at his name, which I find so fitting for the blazing heat in the kitchen (and kind of food he prepares!)—and offered my services. I explained to Danté that although I had never worked in a kitchen, *per se*, I *had* enjoyed years of excellent food in all manner of restaurants and countries, and I was sure that I could be of assistance. Perhaps as a taster and general advisor.

Danté asked me to leave as he was quite busy (he was punching dough for tomorrow's bread) but I think he appreciated my willingness to help. I've already started a list of items to address with him:

1. Do not smoke in the kitchen. Apart from this being a dangerous and disgusting habit, the ash can fall into the food. (Guess who will give the bread a skip tomorrow morning!)

2. Mashed potato is supposed to be white and fluffy, and not taste like grey soap.

3. "Margarine" is not, in fact, an acceptable substitute for butter. In truth, I don't even think of the stuff as edible, but I realise that what is good for the goose is not always good enough for the gander. Etcetera.

4. The same goes for processed cheese. It tastes like plastic. It may even be made out of plastic ... I wouldn't be surprised! As a general rule, you should not feed your customers plastic.

5. Occasional baked goods would be very much appreciated. A good biscuit can form the foundation of a man's happiness, and should not be overlooked.

I have plenty more suggestions, but I think I'll go in with a short list on my first consultation. I don't want to overwhelm the man as he certainly has enough on his plate.

I have also begun to engage with the other guests here at Bridge Gate, and I am finding it a worthwhile cause. Usually I go out of my way to avoid people (as I like to travel alone), but there are a great deal of residents here and most of the time, the company is simply inescapable. I've been chatting to that chap, Locklear, who tends the roses and works in the library mentoring students, and found him to be particularly good company. He is a reader and a thinker (not the cereal box kind), and we seem to get on swimmingly. Whilst discussing Shakespeare—his daughter is studying Romeo and Juliet—he informed me that we have a Shakespearean story of sorts playing out here. Instead of the Montagues and the Capulets, however, we have the "Black-Jacks" and the "White Collars".

Locklear, Smith and I automatically fall into the latter grouping, despite wanting nothing to do with the division. Alas, it appears we have no choice.

(Smith is still a challenge to live with. Have I told you yet that he hoards bananas and sleeps with them under his pillow? He says they help with his gut. The man smells like Monkey World.)

Locklear and I also had a laugh about Danté's name, and I'm glad I'm not the only one who sees the relation between the head cook's infernal kitchen and the nine circles of hell. That got us talking about nominative determinism (the idea that your name has a bearing on your destiny, like a jeweller called 'Stone' or a seamstress named 'Taylor'), and Locklear and I found it amusing that a man with his name would be a resident here. We do certainly appear to share an appreciation for irony. There is also a man in the "BlackJacks" called "Axxe" who walks around with a primitive shiv taped to his right pectoral muscle. Of course, this is not funny at all, but laugh we must, because without humour we would be nothing but unmoored boats in this stormy grey sea we are forced to navigate.

I sometimes wonder how my life would have turned out if I had been born with a different name. I've always detested "Perkins" but now it's stamped on my uniform and everyone here calls me that, so I grin and bear it. It is my real name, after all. It's always been a fascination of mine—names—and I'm forever changing my online profiles. I think it's interesting that people expect you to go by one name your whole life, despite how we humans are constantly changing.

. . .

All in all, I feel that I am starting to settle in a bit. "Bridge Gate" gets an extra star from me, bringing the total to two stars out of five.

Sincerely

Alan Perkins, AKA @PerkyPilgrim

∾

Dear Mr Perkins

While I appreciate your two stars, I must caution you again about sharing too much information on the internet. I see that you have quite a large following. Please remember that what you post on an international review site will remain in the public domain forever. Also keep in mind that it is your responsibility to respect the privacy of your fellow inmates.

While we are on the subject of privacy, it has come to my attention that you spend some time in communal areas *sans* trousers, and have even snagged an appropriate nickname. Please will you refrain from doing so. I don't feel that I need to give further explanation.

Also, our head cook, Danté, has requested you be banned from the kitchen. I don't want to discourage you from thinking of ideas to improve the correctional facility, but perhaps it's best to leave Danté to cook his recipes his way.

Please also exercise caution in what you call the Shakespearean story there in B Wing. I urge you not to take sides or say or do anything that would stoke the conflict between the two groups. It is vital to your safety and others'.

I hope this note is constructive and assists you in keeping the peace.

Sincerely,

Frederick Collis

Director at Bridge Gate Prison

Department of Correctional Services

**Trip Advisor Review: Bridge Gate. 3 out of 5 stars.**

My stay here at Bridge Gate has become a most edifying experience, and for this I award the place another star, despite it's obvious shortcomings in the hospitality department. We may lack baked goods and cultural outings but I am getting to experience some "real life" within these gruel-coloured walls, and what is the point of living if one doesn't get to share these kind of "grass root" encounters?

For example, we have a support group meeting every Thursday, where the resident psychologist comes in and we talk about crime, punishment, and redemption. It sounds like a Russian literary novel by the brothers Karamazov; a Dostoevsky snore-fest, if you will, but let me tell you, it is not!

Hearing about the others' mistakes has made me think about my own. Now I will admit to being difficult in the beginning, stubbornly refusing to confess that I had done anything wrong, but the stories of the other men have suffused me with courage, and helped me to come to terms with the damage I have wreaked in my own life and others.

I'd specifically like to apologise on record and in this public forum to Suzy Dos Santos of The Golden Beach Hotel Group (PTY) LTD. I would send her a direct message but Dr Richards explained to me that Ms Dos Santos does not want to be contacted by me for any reason, even for an apology, and I must respect her wishes. I still hope she stumbles upon this post (isn't that why I share my thoughts here?) but I will not contact her personally. It pains me to admit this, but I have done enough harm. Also, I can't imagine that Ms Dos Santos is the kind of woman who writes to men in prison, so it would feel to me as if the conversation was forever suspended, like a half-healed wound, and that would bother me immensely. As it is, I feel tainted by the harm I have caused, I feel as if my poor life choices will always be with me, just under my skin. A permanent tattoo of self-reproach.

•   •   •

Dr Richards has given us homework. I am to think about my childhood and consider how it has shaped my adult behaviour. I won't beat around the bush: this will be very difficult for me. But I suppose the road to redemption has never been an easy journey.

Signing off now to go for a quick walk in the gardens before girding my loins for one of Dante's dreadful "chicken stews". The other residents snicker and say that he places whole chickens into the grinder to make this particular casserole. I thought they were joking before Smith found what looked like a broken beak in last week's serving. I became (understandably!) upset, even more so than Smith, who just shrugged and carried on slurping up his food. When I get overwhelmed by these thoughts I sing *La Traviata* under my breath, and that helps to calm me down. It helps me to remember that, broken beaks or not, there are still beautiful things in this world.

Sincerely,

Alan Perkins, AKA @PerkyPilgrim

~

Dear Mr Perkins

I am pleased to hear that you are settling down, and that you are having constructive sessions with Dr Richards. I urge you to keep up the good work.

. . .

I will have a word with Danté regarding the chicken casserole.


Sincerely,


Frederick Collis

Director at Bridge Gate Prison

Department of Correctional Services

∾

## Trip Advisor Review: Bridge Gate. 3 out of 5 stars.


I feel as if my consciousness has been smashed open. My soul is now a portal for all the bad memories and traumatic events as they burst forth from my subconscious, shredding my state of mind as they do so. Unwelcome evocations with glinting silver barbs. So much buried trauma now being hoisted up to the light, so much psychic pain. Dr Richards says it is good, good, good, that we are making real progress, but it feels terrible. It feels as though I am being suffocated by the heaviness of the thick black cloud that is the past I have tried so hard to forget. The past I have been running away from for my entire adult life.


Oh, how I wish I could escape the torturous thoughts, scramble away from them, but I know that if I do that, nothing will change.

. . .

Locklear has been a good friend. He listens to me sob about my deplorable childhood and tells me about his daughter at home, who writes to him regularly and keeps him up-to-date with her tumultuous teen life; the excitement and heartache of youth. He is deeply regretful that he cannot be with her as she grows up. He plants a rose bush for every letter he receives. You can tell how very much he loves her, which somehow makes me feel better and worse at the same time.

The "BlackJacks" are becoming more aggressive. They have seen the chink in my armour and make no secret of it. Of course, their taunting only serves to deepen my despair, because when they round on me I'm instantly transported back to when I was a boy being terrorised by the school bullies, who would abuse me in the cruellest ways. It brings flashbacks of being punched in the stomach, and bogwashed, and having my fingers pulled so far back that I was certain they would snap.

I am also made aware of how I grew up to bully others, which will remain a significant sorrow for me for as long as I may live.

Oh, how I long for an escape from this terrible reality. Sometimes I feel as if I would welcome Axxe's shiv being plunged into my aching heart, because then I would be free of the doom and hopelessness. I imagine death with golden winged palms, lifting me out of here and delivering me to a place exuding warmth and light and the welcoming embrace of my imaginary Aunt Daphne and her comforting bosom. It would smell of her sweet perfume and her impossibly light, freshly baked scones, and I would finally be able to forget everything and rest.

· · ·

Perkins

~

Dear Mr Perkins

I'm afraid to inform you that your cell-mate, Smith, has been injured in an altercation in the weights room. We are investigating the incident and will deal with the perpetrators accordingly.

Sincerely,

Frederick Collis

Director at Bridge Gate Prison

Department of Correctional Services

~

**Trip Advisor Review: Bridge Gate. 3 out of 5 stars.**

Oh! I feel like I am being crushed under the grief of this terrible thing. Just as I thought I couldn't possibly feel worse, Smith is almost killed by those reckless barbarians in B Wing. He's been hospitalised with broken ribs and a fractured skull. Locklear has these dark marks under his eyes, as if he has not slept in days. What is the point of living? I see none. Only darkness and despair.

. . .

Perkins

~

Dear Mr Perkins

I understand your concern, and your grief. Dr Richards has informed me that you are making great strides. Keep going!

I'm afraid to say that we have been getting complaints about your belting out Italian opera at the top of your voice. Please try to keep your singing voice to an acceptable level as to not disturb the peace. Also, thank you for making an effort to wear pants.

Smith's condition is improving. His doctor says that if all goes well, he'll be discharged within the next couple of days, so things should be back to normal soon.

Sincerely,

Frederick Collis

Director at Bridge Gate Prison

Department of Correctional Services

~

**Trip Advisor Review: Bridge Gate. 5 out of 5 stars.**

Things are certainly looking up! I am feeling significantly better today after a tough couple of months of "exorcising my demons". Let me tell you, Dante's kitchen has nothing on what was going on inside my head, and Dr Richards is nothing short of a genius. He tore open my psyche and burnt it to the ground. A more humble man, a more whole man, has risen from the ashes.

How desperately paradoxical that it took a trip here for me to wake up to a better life.

Smith is back among us. He is not quite himself, but we are helping him to regain his former health. "Axxe" has been sent to the maximum security wing so we shan't be seeing him again. We are incredibly relieved, although the remaining "Black-Jacks" have made it clear that we shouldn't get too comfortable with the status quo. This morning, in the canteen, one of the brutes lifted his shirt and flashed Axxe's shiv at us. I picked up a bread-roll—hard as a rock, as always—and thought that Dante's cooking might come in handy, after all.

Locklear's roses are in full bloom, and he has recently had a letter from his daughter, which improves his mood for days.

The sky seems more blue, the air smells sweeter. And I ... well, I feel like a new man.

· · ·

Alan Perkins, AKA @PerkyPilgrim

~

Dear Mr Perkins

Please be advised that your early parole application has been approved. Your good behaviour, as well as a convincing report from Dr Richards, secured the approval of the parole board.

It also pleases me to inform you that your application for early parole on behalf of Mister Michael Locklear has also been approved. It was reportedly an easy decision for the board. Apart from your excellent letter, Mr Locklear has been an asset to the facility, working hard in the library and the garden and tutoring his fellow inmates. As far as I know he had no plans to apply at all, so he is in your debt.

You will both be released at the end of this month (Friday the 31$^{st}$ of November), so please make the necessary arrangements.

Congratulations. I have spoken with Danté and he volunteered to bake a cake for your farewell party.

I will make more toilet paper available on the day. (This will be for the traditional 'bunting' at Bridge Gate parties, not because I expect Danté's cake to be problematic.)

·   ·   ·

I will be following your future reviews on Trip Advisor with interest, and I wish you everything of the best.

Sincerely,


Frederick Collis

Director at Bridge Gate Prison

Department of Correctional Services

# ACKNOWLEDGMENTS

Sincere thanks to:

My loyal fans. You have changed my life.

Mike, Keith & Gill for your love and your work.

Mom for always buying my books,

and my generous Patreon supporters.

# ABOUT THE AUTHOR

JT Lawrence is an Amazon bestselling author,
playwright & bookdealer. She lives in Parkview, Johannesburg,
in a house with a red front door.

Follow me on Amazon

Follow me on BookBub

Become a Patreon

www.jt-lawrence.com
janita@pulpbooks.co.za

# DEAR READER

I hope you enjoyed this collection of sticky short stories. I'll be be back with more in 2019.

If you'd like to try some of my other work, you may enjoy my futuristic dystopian thriller series **When Tomorrow Calls.**

*They said they were her parents. They lied.*

*Now they're dead and Kirsten's barcode is next on the list.*

*"The Handmaid's Tale meets Gone Girl."*

*"Oryx and Crake on Speed."*

*"A flat-out addictive series."*

Hope you check it out! And if you do, I'd love to hear from you.

Janita

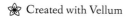 Created with Vellum